Copyright February 2025 by Katie Lane

All rights reserved. Except for use in any review, the reproduction or utilization of this work in whole or in part in any form by any electronic, mechanical or other means, now known or hereinafter invented, including xerography, photocopying and recording, or in any information storage or retrieval system, is forbidden without the written permission of the publisher.

This book is a work of fiction. Names, characters, places, and incidents are a product of the writer's imagination. All rights reserved. Scanning, uploading, and electronic sharing of this book without the permission of the author is unlawful piracy and theft. To obtain permission to excerpt portions of the text, please contact the author at *katie@katielanebooks.com*

Thank you for respecting this author's hard work and livelihood.

Cover Design and Interior Format

© KILLION
 GROUP INC.

Wrangling a WILD TEXAN

HOLIDAY RANCH SEVEN

KATIE LANE

*To my Secret Sisterhoods, Christy,
Sandi, and Cathy,
Aubrey and Tiffany, Gabi and Sienna.
There is no dearer friend than a sister.*

Chapter One

*H*YDROPLANING HAD ALWAYS sounded like a thrilling activity. Like parasailing. Or kite surfing. Or hang gliding. And there was nothing Sunshine Brook Whitlock loved more than a good thrill. She enjoyed walking on the wild side and was up for almost anything: cliff jumping, skydiving, and swimming with sharks. The more daredevil, the more she wanted to try it.

But as her Subaru spun out of control on the icy rain-slick highway, Sunny didn't feel the adrenaline rush of excitement that came with those other thrill-seeking pursuits. She felt the terrifying reality that these could be her last few seconds on the planet Earth.

And seconds weren't nearly enough time to make up for twenty-four years of orneriness.

She might look like the perfect little ray of sunshine, but beneath her sweet smile and innocent brown eyes was a devious devil who had completely hoodwinked her two brothers . . . and everyone else. Mischievous activities drew her like a bee to honey. Over the years, she had become an expert at not getting caught. But now the jig was up and she'd have to face the heavenly jury. With her record, there was no way she was getting past those pearly white gates.

Which meant she was headed straight to—

"Hell!" she yelled as her car careened off the highway. A second later, it slammed into a fence post with a jarring impact that had her body jerking forward.

This was it. She was about to pay for her deception and impulsive, irresponsible behavior. Unfortunately, her brothers would have to pay too. Corbin, who had loved and spoiled her all her life. And Jesse, who loved her just as much, even though they had met only a few months earlier. They would both be devastated by her untimely death. That upset her even more than spending the rest of her days as a deep-fried spicy chicken wing.

But just as she resigned herself to The End of her life story, her seatbelt tightened and the airbag deployed, keeping her from flying through the rain-splattered windshield. She sat there for a stunned moment with her lungs pumping and her heart thumping before she glanced out at the miles of cattle-grazing pasture capped by stormy gray skies.

"I'm alive!" she yelled at the top of her lungs. "I'm alive!" She looked up at the roof of her car. "Thank you, thank you, thank you. I promise to do better and not be so impulsive or ir—"

"Sunshine Whitlock."

She startled at the authoritative female voice that echoed through the interior of her car. She swallowed hard. Obviously, God wasn't buying her oath. While she quaked with reverent fear, she also felt vindicated.

She'd always suspected God was a woman.

"This is vehicle assistance," the voice said.

Or maybe not.

"We were notified that your airbags deployed. Are you okay?"

"Oh!" She laughed with relief. "Yes, I'm fine, but you might want to send—" Before she could finish there was a frantic tapping on her side window. She turned to see a completely drenched and hysterical teenage girl.

"Oh my God!" Sophie Mitchell's muffled voice came through the glass. "Are you okay? I'm so sorry. I only glanced at my phone for a second. Just a second. I didn't mean to swerve into your lane. I'm so sorry . . . so, so sorry." She covered her face with her hands and started sobbing.

Sunny quickly rolled down the window. "Hey, now. I'm fine, honey. Just fine. Are you okay?"

Sophie lowered her hands. The few times Sunny had been around the teenager, she'd noticed Sophie had a heavy hand with makeup. Between the rain and crying, most of that makeup was dripping down her face. Which made Sunny want to hand her a tissue . . . and give her a quick tutorial on makeup application.

"I'm okay," Sophie sniffed. "But I won't be for long. My uncle is going to kill me. Kill me!"

Just the mention of Sophie's uncle had an image popping into Sunny's head. An image of a man with hair the exact color of the onyx necklace she hadn't been about to resist buying when she'd been living in Paris and intense eyes the deep amber of expensive French champagne. Those features were accompanied by a movie star handsome face and a hard, muscled body that would send any woman racing for her vibrator. Sunny had gone through numerous AA batteries fantasizing about Sophie's uncle.

Of course, in her fantasies, he was nice.

In real life, he was a grumpy bumpkin.

"Ms. Whitlock?" The vehicle assistance woman cut into Sunny's thoughts. "Do we need to send emergency assistance?"

Since the front of her car was wrapped around a fence post and the engine made a strange grinding sound, emergency assistance was definitely needed. But before she could speak, she glanced at Sophie and saw the pleading look in her amber eyes.

It was hard not to sympathize with the girl. Sunny didn't know the full story of why Sophie was living with her grumpy uncle, but she did know what it felt like to be dumped on some relative who didn't really want you. She and Corbin had been dumped more times than she could count, which explained all her mischievous behavior. She'd needed an outlet for her hurt and anger.

She couldn't blame Sophie for needing the same.

She gave her an encouraging smile as she answered the vehicle assistance operator.

"No need to send help. It's just a little fender bender—something I can turn in to my insurance. You don't need to call 911." Especially when Sheriff Decker Carson was a friend of Corbin's. While Corbin was a loving brother, he had a tendency to overreact. He would not be happy Sunny had driven from Houston to Wilder in an ice storm and gotten into an accident. Especially when he had informed her of the impending storm and told her not to come until the following day.

But some things were worth braving a storm.

Like loyalty to the Sisterhood.

Tonight, the Holiday Secret Sisterhood was having a meeting and Sunny had spent her entire life wanting a sister. After Corbin and Jesse had married the Holiday twins, Sunny now had six. Six sisters to drink Mimi's homemade elderberry wine with and skinny-dip at Cooper Springs with and confide her deepest, darkest secrets to. Not that she had confided her deepest, darkest secrets yet. But she hoped to. She hoped sisters would understand her much better than her brothers did.

"Let us know if you do need help," the operator said.

"Will do!" Once she hung up, Sunny turned to Sophie. "Get in out of the rain while I call roadside assistance."

Sophie sat in the passenger seat and shivered while Sunny made the call. Unfortunately, it would be hours before roadside assistance could send someone out to tow her car. Since patience had never been her virtue, she decided to leave the car for the tow guy to deal with while she caught a ride to Corbin and Belle's house with Sophie.

At least that was the plan until she glanced out the rain-splattered windshield and saw a dark blob approaching. With each swipe of the wipers, the blob grew more and more defined. Soon, she realized it was a horse and rider.

Since they were on the Holiday Ranch, it could be any number of people. Hank Holiday, the patriarch of the Holiday family. Darla, his wife. Mimi, his mama—or probably not since Mimi rarely rode anymore. One of the six Holiday sisters. Or one of the sisters' husbands—Sunny's brothers included.

But it turned out to be none of those people.

"Oh, shit! That's Uncle Reid." Sophie turned to Sunny. "Please don't tell him about me texting and driving. He'll be mad enough that I took his truck without permission. If he finds out I ran you off the road, he'll put me on restriction for life."

Sunny stared at Sophie. "You took your uncle's truck without permission?"

Sophie sputtered. "U-U-Uhh . . . I wasn't planning on being gone long. I was just gonna practice driving before the storm hit."

"Practice driving? You don't have your driver's license?"

"Well, no, but that's not my fault. In order to get my license, I need to have a ton of driving hours with a licensed driver and Uncle Reid just doesn't have the time. So I've been—"

"Driving by yourself and forging his name." Damn, this teenage girl really did remind Sunny of herself. She'd forged her guardians' names on more than one occasion. But that didn't make it right. She blew out her breath. "Your uncle *should* put you on restriction for the rest of your life. That way you might stay alive."

"So you're gonna tell him?"

Sunny glanced out the windshield and watched as Reid rode up on the beautiful chestnut horse. He looked like he belonged in an old western . . . or a girl's wet dream. His rain-dripping Stetson was pulled low and he wore a long duster that flapped around his muscled legs as he effortlessly swung down from the horse. He turned in the direction of his truck that was parked on the side of the road a few yards away before his head swiveled to them. Sunny couldn't see his face, but she could feel the intensity of his gaze. He headed toward them in long ground-eating strides. When he pulled open Sophie's door, his champagne eyes were filled with concern.

"Soph! Are you okay? Are you hurt?"

"I'm fine, Uncle Reid."

His gaze snapped over to Sunny and she experienced the same feeling she always experienced when he looked at her—like she was sitting in front of a really hot principal who was about to discipline her. "Are you hurt, Ms. Whitlock?"

She held out her arms. "Right as rain."

His gaze swept over her and her breathlessness grew. "So what happened?"

Sophie sent her a pleading look. As much as the teenager deserved to get into a whole mess of trouble, Sunny couldn't bring herself to tattle. It wasn't like teenagers didn't do stupid things. Sunny had stolen more than one car, driven without a driver's license, and texted while driving. So she couldn't very well point fingers.

She pinned on a bright smile. "What happened was I got a little too big for my britches and thought I could drive much faster on a slick highway than I could." That much was true. She had been going a little too fast. Of course, the truck coming straight at her hadn't helped. "I hydroplaned and ran off the road. Sophie stopped to make sure I was okay."

The concerned look left Reid's eyes to be replaced with an emotion that was easy to read: anger. And someone being angry with her was not something Sunny was used to. People loved her. Or if not loved her, at least liked her. And why wouldn't they? She was the life of every party. The beacon of light on the darkest days. The sweet little ol' gal who made people smile. In fact, making people smile was what she did best.

Just not with Reid Mitchell.

His face seemed to be frozen in a perpetual frown whenever she was around. No matter how bright and funny she was, he always looked at her like she was an annoying pest he had repeatedly tried to exterminate without luck.

Today was no exception.

"Your recklessness could have killed someone," he snapped.

"No, Uncle Reid," Sophie jumped in. "Sunny was nowhere close to hitting me. She only skidded a little and I braked fast so I wouldn't hit her."

"A little?" He looked at the front of the car hugging the fence post before his attention returned to Sunny, his eyes glittering with suppressed anger.

Just like that, Sunny felt like she'd just jumped out of a plane at twenty thousand feet. She felt weightless, breathless, and . . . extremely turned on. All she could think about was Reid bending her over those muscular wrangler-encased thighs and giving her a much-deserved spanking.

"Does your car run?"

His question snapped Sunny out of her naughty-girl fantasy and made her realize that her engine had quit. She turned the key to restart it and there was a loud grinding noise like a forgotten spoon in a garbage disposal. She sent the grumpy cowboy a smile.

"I guess that would be a no."

His lips pressed into a firm line. "Get in the truck. I'll drive you to Corbin and Belle's house. I'm assuming that's where you were headed."

"Yes, but you don't need to drive me. I can walk. It's not that far."

He snorted. "I'm sure my boss would love it if I let his sister walk home in a rainstorm. Now grab your stuff and get in the truck. You too, Soph."

Sunny had never let men tell her what to do—not even her two brothers. But before she could tell him to go to hell, he took off his rain slicker and held it out for Sophie. Sunny didn't know if it was the sweet way he enfolded his niece in the coat or the way the rain turned his white T-shirt transparent that made her follow his orders.

Probably the T-shirt.

By the time he helped Sophie into his truck and sent the horse back to the stables, it was nothing more than wet tissue paper. When he walked over to her, holding his duster over both their heads as she got her suitcase out of the trunk, she couldn't help staring like a spectator at a bodybuilding competition. With his arms raised, his biceps popped into orange-sized knots, his pectorals flexed into hard, nipple-topped slabs, and his stomach was a tempting washboard that begged to be strummed.

"Stop."

The gruff command had Sunny's gaze snapping up to Reid's face. An angry and annoyed face. "Stop what?"

"You know what, Ms. Whitlock. That innocent act isn't going to work with me. I know your type."

"Really? Exactly what is my type?"

He started to say something, but then snapped his mouth shut and shook his head. "Never mind." He handed her the duster and took her suitcase from her before turning for the truck. Unwilling to let him brush her off so easily, she hurried after him and grabbed his arm.

It was like grabbing on to a bolt of lightning. As soon as her fingers curved around his muscled forearm, an electric current raced through her, lighting up her entire body like a thousand-watt light bulb. She would have thought she was the only one who felt it if his breath hadn't sucked in and his pupils hadn't dilated. Before she could get over her reaction—and his—he jerked away.

"I think I need to make things perfectly clear, Ms. Whitlock. I'm not interested. Do you understand me? Not only because you're my boss's little sister and I don't want to get fired, but also because you're trouble. Trouble is the last thing I need right now. So stay away from me . . . and Sophie." He turned and headed to his truck, carelessly tossing her suitcase into the bed.

Any other woman would have felt embarrassed. Or annoyed. Or angry. Sunny felt none of those things. As she stood there in the cold drizzle and watched him climb into the cab of his truck and slam the door hard, she only felt one thing.

Challenged.

And Sunshine Brook Whitlock had never been able to ignore a challenge in her life.

Chapter Two

REID MITCHELL'S PLANS for his life had never included being a parent to a belligerent teenager. He had never wanted kids. Kids were chaos in pint-sized bodies. Reid had never liked chaos. He liked things quiet and simple.

Which probably explained why he had never gotten along with his sister.

Bree was chaos with a capital *C* and had caused their mama more than her fair share of grief. She had smoked and taken drugs and gotten kicked out of school. At seventeen, she'd run off with some loser and never looked back. Occasionally, he or his mama had gotten a call from her saying she'd broken up with another deadbeat and needed money for her and Sophie—the daughter of one of those deadbeats—to start over. But mostly she lived her life and let Reid live his. When Mama passed away, he'd boxed up things he thought Bree might like and sent them to Oklahoma City where she had been living at the time. She didn't reply. No thank you. No go to hell. Nothing. He didn't hear a peep out of her until she called to tell him she had terminal cancer.

First, he'd felt stunned, like someone had sucker punched him without any warning at all. Then he'd felt sad. Overwhelmingly sad. Finally, he'd felt angry. Angry that she hadn't even said goodbye to him when she'd left home and yet here she was calling to ask if he'd take care of her kid. Didn't she have a boyfriend? A close friend or neighbor? Anyone would make a better father than her loner brother who preferred horses and cows to people.

But it turned out that the last few years of her life she had been as much of a loner as he was. There had been no boyfriend. No friends. He was the only one she could ask. He thought about refusing, but while she had been the irresponsible daughter, he had been the responsible son—the son who kept his room spotless, did all his homework, and worked a job after school to help his single mama pay the bills. The one who called the landlord to fix the leak in the roof and mowed the weeds when they got too high. The one who bought groceries and learned how to cook healthy meals for their diabetic mama. The one who had been sitting in his truck outside the quarantined hospital when the doctor had called him to say she'd passed away from covid.

As much as he wanted to, he couldn't ignore his sister's plea.

So he'd quit his job as foreman for a ranch outside of Amarillo and headed to Wichita Falls where his sister and niece had been living. The money he'd put away as a down payment for his own ranch had quickly been used to pay his sister's mounting bills.

Five and half months later, Bree was gone and Reid had no job, no money, and custody of a belligerent, mourning teenager. He was completely clueless on how to deal with Sophie. He had never understood women. He still didn't. He didn't understand why his mama fell in love with a married man and had two kids with him. He didn't understand why Bree had gotten with clones of their philandering daddy. He certainly didn't understand why Sophie had stolen his truck and gone for a joyride in the middle of a rainstorm.

Woman were frustrating as hell and the woman sitting in the passenger seat chattering away like she hadn't just been driving recklessly and could have killed an innocent young girl was no different.

". . . I swear he looked just like Ryan Gosling. He was sitting at the table sipping his Starbucks and scrolling through his phone. I thought to myself, I can walk out of this coffee shop and spend the rest of my life wondering or I can get up enough courage to walk over and ask. So I walked right up to him and said, 'Hey, where's Barbie?' When he glanced up, I knew immediately that he wasn't Ryan. But he was still a pretty cute guy. He flashed a nice smile and said, 'I'm not really into Barbie, but I do have a thing for Strawberry Shortcake.'"

"Who's Strawberry Shortcake?" Sophie asked from the back seat.

"Good question," Sunny said. "I didn't know either. So the guy pulled up a picture on his phone and showed me. She's a cute little doll with red hair. Sam—that was the guy's name—said his big sister had one. And I guess he loved to carry it around when he was a toddler and give it kisses. Now he has a thing for redheads."

If Reid had been participating in the conversation, he would have pointed out that Sunny's hair wasn't red. It was the color of a newly minted penny. Or a polished copper tub. Or the last hint of sunset before it dipped below the horizon.

Sophie clutched her chest. "Aww, that is so sweet. Did he ask you out on a date?"

"As a matter of fact, he did and I accepted."

It figured. Airhead Ken was definitely Sunny's type.

"So he's your steady boyfriend?" Sophie asked.

"No. I don't really do steady boyfriends."

Reid could feel her gaze burning a hole into the side of his face, but he refused to glance over—just like he'd refused to look at her since she'd climbed into his truck. He might not understand women, but he was smart enough to know the ones he needed to stay away from.

Sunny Whitlock was a woman he needed to stay away from.

Far away from.

From what he'd heard, she was as flighty as his sister. She moved around a lot, had never been in a serious relationship, and didn't have a job—at least not a real job. She painted country landscapes and lived off her brother's money.

That brother just happened to be Reid's boss.

Hallie Holiday might run the Holiday Ranch, but Corbin Whitlock owned the large spread. While he stayed out of ranch business, there was little doubt he'd step in if one of the ranch's employees was messing around with his little sister. Corbin was a fair man, but he wore blinders when it came to Sunny. She had bamboozled him and all the other Holidays into believing she was this sweet little ray of sunshine. But having grown up with his sister, Reid knew trouble when he saw it.

He needed this job. Not only because it paid well, but also because Wilder was a nice place to live. The townsfolk had welcomed him and Sophie with open arms. The high school football coach, Jace Carson, had made Sophie his kicker and given her lots of encouragement. Mimi and Darla Holiday were constantly bringing them casseroles and pies. And once Corbin and Belle's house had been completed, Corbin had moved his old mobile home to the ranch for Reid and Sophie to live in so they wouldn't have to continue to live in Reid's small travel trailer.

The Holidays were good folks. Reid wasn't going to screw up the heaven-sent situation he'd landed in because of a little sexual attraction.

And as much as he wanted to deny it, he *was* sexually attracted to Sunny.

But what man wouldn't be?

She was a stunningly beautiful woman with a

mane of strawberry blond hair and deep chocolate brown eyes that any man would be happy to drown in. When she'd sat down next to him at the Holidays' Thanksgiving feast and turned those pretty eyes on him, he couldn't even string two words together . . . until she'd punched him hard in the arm and knocked some sense into him. At first, he'd thought it was her way of being friendly. After all, she had two rough and tumble brothers. But when she continued to do it all through the meal, he'd decided she was just a little crazy.

Beautiful, crazy women needed to be avoided at all costs.

"Reid?" The way Sunny said his name made his gut tighten. "Umm . . . do you think you could maybe not tell my brother exactly what happened."

"Please, Uncle Reid," Sophie pleaded. "Don't tattle on Sunny. Nobody was hurt."

He kept his gaze on the dirt road that led to the Whitlocks' house and refused to notice the way Sunny's wet jean skirt had inched up her tanned thighs. "But they could have been. And I don't keep secrets." He glanced in the rearview mirror at his niece. "And don't think you've gotten off, Soph. You're in big trouble for taking my truck without permission."

Sophie released a frustrated groan he'd heard at least a hundred times in the last few months and shot him a belligerent look. He wanted to say something else, something fatherly and wise. But he wasn't fatherly and he certainly wasn't wise where kids were concerned. Now if she had been a cow or horse, things would be different. He could handle any animal on a ranch.

Teenage girls?

Not at all.

Holding in his own groan of frustration, he pulled in front of Corbin and Belle's house before jumping out. When he came around the front of his truck, Sunny was waiting for him. Again, he refused to notice the way her wet shirt clung to her full breasts or the outline of her pebbled nipples.

"Okay, I get it," she said. "You're upset that Sophie could have been hurt and you want to make me pay for being so irresponsible. But I'm not a fifteen-year-old kid that Corbin is going to discipline. He'll yell a little, but he'll be more upset and worried than angry. And I hate to worry my brother. So let's just keep what happened between us, shall we? We can just say I had car trouble and you came to my rescue. That will earn you much more brownie points with my brother than telling him the truth." She hesitated, biting down on her plump bottom lip, then releasing it in a slow, slick slide. "And as far as paying for my actions goes, I'll be happy to take whatever discipline you want to dish out."

There was no denying the sexual innuendo. Or the reaction his body had to it. Desire slammed into him and his cock hardened so quickly he felt lightheaded. But he had spent his entire life ignoring his body's fickle desires. He refused to be his father. Or his sister.

He was stronger than that.

"I don't think you'd like the way I dish out discipline, Ms. Whitlock."

He expected the amused twinkle to leave her eyes. He did not expect it to be replaced with heat. So much heat that those eyes looked like two steamy cups of strong coffee. Before he could get over her unexpected reaction to his words, Corbin came out the front door with a tiger-striped kitten tucked in his arm and a huge fuzzy dog bouncing around his heels.

"Sunny?"

She sent Reid a pleading look before she pinned on a smile and turned to her brother. "Surprise!"

The dog raced down the steps and jumped on her, knocking her back into Reid. She giggled as the hairy beast licked her face, completely unaware of the sexual turmoil the brush of her lithe body caused. He steadied her and quickly stepped away as she greeted the dog.

"Hey, Gilley, you big ol' ball of fur." She gave him a good ear scratch before she pushed him down and headed up the porch steps. "And how's my sweet Tay-Tay?" She stroked the kitten's head. "As spoiled as always, I see."

"Speaking of spoiled." Corbin shifted the kitten to his other arm and pulled Sunny in for a tight hug. "I thought I told you to stay in Houston until after the storm. You're soaking wet." He glanced at Reid. "Why is Reid bringing you home?"

Reid started to explain, but Sunny cut him off.

"I had car trouble." When Corbin's eyebrows

lowered, she held up a hand. "I know I should have heeded your warning and waited until tomorrow to drive here." She flashed him a wide-eyed, innocent look. "But I just missed you and Jesse and my new sisters so much that I couldn't stay away a second longer."

"You wouldn't miss us if you moved here like we all want you to."

She swatted his arm. "Now you know it wouldn't be any fun to live in the same town as my overprotective big brothers, Cory."

Corbin glanced up at the gray skies that were still spitting rain and scowled. "You need to be protected. I'm surprised you didn't get in an accident in this weather."

"Here safe and sound." She shot Reid a bright smile. "Thanks to Reid coming to my rescue. You should give the man a raise for being such a sweet hero."

Corbin laughed. "If he had to put up with your chatter all the way here, he probably deserves one." He smiled at Reid. "Thank you for coming to her rescue, Reid. I'll call a tow truck and have them pick up her car."

"I already did," Sunny said. "Now if you're through being the overprotective brother, I need to change out of these wet clothes." Her gaze returned to Reid. "And you need to get out of your wet clothes too, Reid." Her eyes ran over him like a steam iron set on high before they lifted. "I wouldn't want you to catch a nasty cold all because of little ol' me." With one more sul try look that heated him from the inside out, she turned and headed into the house.

Once she was gone, Corbin shook his head. "She's a handful that one. I hope she didn't talk your ear off on the drive over."

This was where Reid should tell the truth. But it was too late for that. Now, in order to tell the truth, he'd have to call Sunny a liar. Somehow he didn't think that would ingratiate him to Corbin.

"No, sir. She was fine." He walked back to the truck to get her suitcase. It was expensive leather and covered in the designer's logo. Reid's luggage was Glad trash bags. Just another reminder of how different he and Sunny were and why he needed to stay far away from her.

"Everything okay with your new home?" Corbin asked as Reid set the luggage down on the porch.

"Yes, sir. I sure appreciate you getting it all set up for us. Making sure we have water and electricity couldn't have been cheap. I'd be happy to repay you for any costs."

"We had to run lines for the house as well so it wasn't a big deal."

Reid glanced at the two-story home with its wraparound porch and brand-new everything. It was huge, but similar to the Holidays' big farmhouse, still homey.

"It turned out real nice, Mr. Whitlock."

"It was all Belle. She knew exactly what she wanted and I just kept my mouth shut and signed the checks." His gaze moved to Gilley who was jumping up on Reid's truck. "Gilley! Get down from—" He cut off when the window rolled down and Sophie stuck her head out to greet the dog. "Hey, Sophie! I didn't realize you were with your uncle. Get down, Gilley. I'm sure Sophie doesn't want dog slobbers."

Sophie scratched the dog's floppy ears. "It's okay. I love dogs." Reid was surprised. He hadn't thought his niece liked much of anything.

"So how's school?" Corbin asked.

"Okay."

It was the same answer she gave Reid every time he asked. While Reid would usually nod and go on about his business, Corbin didn't let it go.

"It's tough adjusting to a new school, isn't it? Everyone is already in their friend groups and you feel like the odd one out."

To Reid's surprise, Sophie nodded sadly. "Yeah."

Corbin sent Sophie an understanding look. "Believe me, I get it. Sunny and I are experts on moving to new schools and feeling like the odd ones out. So if you ever want to talk about it, I'm here."

Sophie shared one of her rare smiles. "Thanks, Mr. Whitlock."

Corbin winked. "Call me Corbin. I've told your uncle the same thing, but he refuses to listen."

"He's stubborn like that."

Corbin laughed and glanced over at Reid. "I'm figuring that out."

On the drive back to the trailer, Reid had planned on lecturing Sophie about taking his truck without permission. But now he had a bigger concern.

"You feel like the odd man out at school?" He glanced at her in the rearview mirror.

She huffed and flopped back in the seat out of his line of vision. "Please don't make it into a big deal."

"But if you're feeling ostracized at school, it is a big deal, Soph. You told me everything was okay."

She kicked the back of his seat so hard that he jerked forward and his seatbelt tightened. "Well, it's not okay. Nothing is okay. But I'm not going to talk about it with someone who never understood my mom and will never understand me."

Reid wanted to deny it, but couldn't. She was right. He hadn't understood her mom. And he certainly didn't understand Sophie. He had spent his life being an introvert who preferred his own company. He'd had friends, but never close ones. The same was true with girlfriends. He'd dated, but never seriously. When women got to close, he'd broken things off.

Now he had this person he needed to get close to. And he just didn't know how.

He squeezed the steering wheel in frustration and said the only thing that came to mind. "You want frozen pizza for dinner?"

CHAPTER THREE

THE SECRET SISTERHOOD meeting was usually held in the hayloft of the Holiday's big ol' red barn. As far as Sunny was concerned, it was the ideal spot to cozy up with all six sisters and share secrets. Being that she was the newest member, Sunny felt obligated to be the first sharer. She definitely had a lot of secrets she'd been keeping.

Unfortunately, once Sweetie, the oldest sister and president of the club, called the meeting to order and asked if there was anything that needed to be discussed, Sunny struggled to reveal the sad truths about her own life and instead blurted out someone else's.

"Sophie Mitchell stole her uncle's truck and ran me off the road today!"

The sisters looked stunned—and probably more by Sunny's sudden outburst than the actual information—before Liberty laughed.

"That sounds like something I would do." She glanced at Belle sitting next to her in the hayloft. It still boggled Sunny's mind how much the Holiday twins looked alike. They were both gorgeous with their raven hair and Holiday green eyes. Although, interestingly enough, as their pregnancies progressed, their bodies were starting to look different. Liberty's hips had widened and she had a noticeable baby bump while Belle was barely showing. "Remember when we stole Daddy's truck and went for a joyride, Belly?"

"You stole Daddy's truck," Belle corrected.

Liberty huffed. "Po-ta-to po-tah-to. You were with me."

"Only because you needed a voice of reason with you—not that you listened to me when you ran straight into that ditch."

"You were lucky neither one of you got hurt," Cloe said. Clover Holiday Remington was the soft-spoken, protective sister. Her green eyes filled with concern when she turned to Sunny. "Are you okay?" Once Sunny gave the sisters all the details, Cloe looked even more concerned. "Are you sure you got it across to Sophie the seriousness of what she did?"

Sunny had spent the entire afternoon worried about the same thing. Which was probably why she'd blurted the truth out. "I tried to, but what if I didn't? What if she drives and texts again and gets in a serious accident? It will be all my fault because I didn't want her to get into trouble. But maybe she needed to be severely disciplined by Reid."

"Severely?" Hallie laughed. "Reid? He's a big ol' pussycat."

"He doesn't seem like a pussycat to me. He seems more like a grumpy lion with a thorn in his paw." Or a sexy panther who made Sunny weak in the knees.

"He's just quiet and a bit of a loner." Hallie tossed Sunny a can of Sprite from the mini cooler she'd brought up to the hayloft. Since they now had two nursing mothers and three pregnant women in the group, they no longer drank Mimi's homemade elderberry wine at the meetings.

As she popped open the can, Sunny couldn't help feeling a little disappointed. She had spent years dreaming about what the sisters did in their secret meetings. Her wild imagination had conjured up blood rituals, male voodoo doll stabbings, and lots of shared naughty secrets. But so far, besides skinny-dipping at Cooper Springs, the meetings had been pretty tame. Which explained why Sunny hadn't shared any of her wild exploits or best-kept secrets. She worried the sisters would toss her out of the club if they found out all the mischief she'd gotten into over the years and all the lies she'd told her brothers—and them.

And as tame as the meetings were, Sunny loved being part of the Sisterhood and a group of women who loved and supported each other. Hopefully, in time, Sunny would get the courage to share more truths.

"I think Reid is really trying to be a good guardian to Sophie," Hallie continued. "He's been asking me a lot of questions about teenage girls. Poor guy. It can't be easy to deal with a grieving teenager while you're doing your own grieving." Tears entered her eyes, which was completely unusual for tough Hallie. "I don't know what I'd do if I lost a sister."

Sunny stared at her. "Sophie's mama died?" She had thought her mama just hadn't wanted to raise her. She knew all about parents not wanting to raise their own kids.

Hallie nodded. "I don't know all the details. Reid isn't exactly the sharing type."

"Poor Sophie." Noelle entered the conversation. She was the youngest Holiday sister and the sister Sunny was the closest to. Probably because she was a bit of a fibber like Sunny. Noelle had fake dated Casey Remington, all to appease her thousands of social media followers. Sunny was only lying to her brothers . . . and the Secret Sisterhood . . . and the townsfolk. She cringed as Noelle continued. "I just feel for that sweet thing. Sophie looks so unhappy every time I see her. Now I get it. She's grieving her mama. Not to mention that she had to move to a new town and a new school. High school can be so brutal."

Hallie rolled her eyes. "Please don't get into the entire thing about Casey bullying you, Elle. Especially when you ended up marrying your bully and are living happily ever after on a ranch bigger than this one." Noelle had recently married Casey, who owned the Remington Ranch with his father, Sam, and brother, Rome—Cloe's husband. Now she and Casey were expecting their first child. It really was a happily ever after. Sunny couldn't help feeling a little jealous.

Noelle always seemed to get everything a girl could want.

All the Holiday sisters did.

Which explained why Sunny had been infatuated with them ever since she and Corbin had arrived in Wilder to live with their uncle. Or more like been forced on their uncle like unwanted baggage. Sophie wasn't unwanted baggage. Her mama had no choice in leaving her. But Reid had had a choice. He could have refused to take his niece and left her to foster care. Instead, he had accepted the responsibility and seemed to care enough to ask Hallie for advice. Sunny's uncle hadn't given a crap about her and Corbin. The only reason he'd taken them in was because of the money her daddy sent him monthly. Money he had spent on booze and lottery tickets.

Reid might be grumpy, but at least he was trying. Still, Noelle's comments about high school had Sunny worried. High school *had* been brutal—at least for her. While she hadn't been bullied, she had been ostracized as the weird new girl who carried her sketchpad wherever she went. She couldn't stand the thought of the same thing happening to Sophie.

"Does Sophie have any friends?" she asked.

Liberty scratched her growing belly and shook her head. "Not that I have seen, but I don't hang around with teenagers much." She glanced at Noelle. "What about you, Elle? Don't all the kids come in for muffins after school?"

"Yes, but not Sophie. She only comes in with Reid and she never looks happy about it."

"She might just be a moody loner like Hallie was," Sweetie said.

"I was not a moody loner!" Hallie snapped. "I just wasn't trying to win Miss Popularity like you and Lib." Her brows knitted. "But maybe Sunny is struggling to make friends at school. I'll talk to Jace and have him keep an eye out." Hallie's husband was the football coach at the high school. If anyone could spy on Sophie at school, it would be Jace.

"Good idea, Hal," Sweetie said. "Once you find out, text us on the sister loop."

"And what then?" Sunny asked. "If she doesn't have any friends, how can we help her? It's not like we can fix her situation at school."

Cloe nodded. "That's true. But maybe we can give her support outside of school."

"Great idea, Cloe," Belle said. "We could be like her big sisters."

"I hate to rain on your big sister parade, Belly," Liberty said. "But just when are we going to find the time to do that? We have obstetrician appointments and all our events here and in Austin and Houston. Not to mention, I have to help Jesse get the bed-and-breakfast ready for its grand opening. And don't you and Corbin still have to finish decorating your new house? I just can't see us having any spare time."

Belle sighed. "You're right. Corbin has already asked me to cut back."

"And you should," Cloe said. "You, Libby, and Noelle will need every ounce of spare energy for when your babies get here. Autumn Grace is over four months old and I still don't have time to shave my legs."

"I think I got to shave one armpit . . . a week ago," Sweetie said. "Thank God Decker is as tired as I am and doesn't notice."

Hallie scrunched her face in disgust. "All it takes is one sisterhood meeting to scare me away from having kids."

Sweetie laughed. "Kids are the best, Hal. They just don't leave much time for anything else."

"So I guess it's up to me and Sunny to be Sophie's big sisters?" Hallie heaved a sigh. "Fine. Maybe I'll see if she wants to help out on the ranch after school. That might improve her and Reid's relationship as well. And maybe you could teach her how to paint, Sun."

Sunny got the same anxious feeling she always got when anyone brought up her painting. Luckily, she had an excuse for why she couldn't teach Sophie to paint. "I wish I could, but I'm only staying a few days."

The sisters all exchanged looks before Hallie spoke. "That's right. I forgot. I guess that leaves me being the sole big sister. Now if that's all we need to talk about, I vote we adjourn the meeting. I have a cute coach waiting for me."

"I second that," Cloe said.

Sweetie jumped in. "All those in fav—"

Sunny was so disappointed about the meeting being cut short, she couldn't help blurting out once again, "But it's a full moon!" She pointed at the cloudy skies out the open hatch doors of the hayloft. "You can't see it, but it's full tonight. I checked. Isn't it a rule that we have to go skinny-dipping at Cooper Springs on a full moon?"

"We don't always skinny-dip on a full moon," Liberty said. "Just when the weather is nice. It's still a little to chilly for this sister."

Sunny wouldn't mind swimming in an ice block as long as she got to do something exciting with the Sisterhood. But she could tell by everyone's faces that they didn't feel the same way.

"You're right, Libby." She smiled and tapped herself on the head. "I don't know what I was thinking. Y'all need to get home to your sweet babies and good-lookin' men."

When everyone stood and headed toward the hayloft ladder, Noelle came over and gave her a hug. "We'll go skinny-dipping next full-moon meeting. I promise. And it's not like we won't get to hang out together tomorrow night."

"Tomorrow night?" Sunny looked at her with surprise. "Are we having a sister get-together?"

Noelle's cheeks turned pink. "No . . . uhh . . ." Before she could continue, Hallie came over and hooked an arm around her sister—or more like put her in a headlock. "Come on, Elle. It's obvious we're both too tired to think straight."

"Sunny!" Belle called. "We need to get home before it starts to rain."

Since Corbin and Belle's new house was only a hop, skip, and a jump from the Holidays' house, Belle and Sunny had walked to the meeting. Because of the weather, Corbin hadn't been keen on the idea. So Sunny wasn't surprised to find her brother waiting outside the barn with an umbrella.

"How did the meeting go?"

Belle lifted up on her toes and kissed his cheek. "Didn't trust us to walk home in the dark, did you?"

"It's not about trust. It's about you two running off without being prepared." He popped open the umbrella before clicking on the flashlight in his hand.

Belle laughed and hooked her arm through his. "My chivalrous, overprotective villain."

Corbin smiled down at her with a dopey look. "You mean a whipped hero who would do just about anything for his lady?" He glanced at Sunny and winked. "Ladies." He held out his other arm. "So what mischief did the sisters get into tonight?"

Sunny slipped her arm through his and sighed. "No mischief."

None at all.

Once they got back to the house, Sunny talked Corbin and Belle into watching one of her favorite movies, *The Shape of Water*. But before the cleaning lady could fall in love with the amphibian guy, both Corbin and Belle were sound asleep with Gilley and Tay-Tay cuddled between them. Since she had lost interest in the movie too, Sunny turned off the television, tucked a throw blanket around them, and headed out to the front porch.

The storm had passed and the temperature had returned to the moderate night temps of early March in Texas—obviously, Liberty had just used the cold as an excuse to cut the meeting short. Which was weird. Sunny had heard stories of the sisters skinny-dipping in much colder temperatures. And what was the get-together Noelle had been talking about? Had the sisters planned something tomorrow night and Noelle had messed up by inviting her? As much as the Holiday sisters had welcomed Sunny into their fold, she knew she was still the outsider—the one with not a speck of Holiday blood running through her veins.

She didn't know why she felt so upset. She should be used to it by now. She had spent her entire life being the outsider—the new kid who never quite fit in. When Corbin had been in elementary school with her, it hadn't been so bad. They'd had each other. But when he had moved to middle school, she'd had to brave school all by herself. Most of her teachers had been understanding and nice. It was on the playgrounds and during lunch when she felt the most alone . . . and terrified.

Bullies preyed on kids who sat all alone looking scared.

So Sunny learned to hide her fear behind a bright smile and her sketchpad. She acted like she was perfectly fine sitting by herself under a tree or at a cafeteria table, drawing away.

She'd done the same thing every time her parents split up and she and Corbin were pawned off with another relative. She had smiled, with her sketchpad tucked under her arm and her trash bag of clothes at her feet, and waved until her mama's or daddy's car had driven out of sight. Unlike Corbin, who had grown angrier and angrier each time they'd been dropped off, Sunny had remained cheerful and positive.

There was no use getting angry over something you couldn't change.

Or holding grudges.

While Corbin refused to even talk to their parents, Sunny called them once a week and sent them money every month. If she ever felt a twinge of bitterness or anger about her past life, she pushed it way down deep and did something exciting.

She glanced at the full moon hanging in the starry sky and smiled.

Like night skinny-dipping.

By the time she reached Cooper Springs, the full moon had risen even higher in the sky. It reflected in the dark pool of water like a rippling sheet of gold satin. Sunny didn't hesitate to strip off her clothes and dive in.

Liberty was right. The temperature outside might not be that cold, but the water was freezing. She swam vigorously for a few minutes to get her body acclimated before she floated onto her back and looked up at the moon.

Beneath its huge glowing magnificence, she felt small and insignificant . . . or maybe she'd always felt small and insignificant. Maybe that was why she tried so hard to be liked. She wanted to prove she mattered. But as she floated there, she realized she didn't matter. Everyone seemed to be moving on with their lives just fine without her. The Holiday sisters had their new husbands and babies . . . and each other. Corbin had his investment business, the ranch, Belle, and a baby on the way. Jesse had the bed-and-breakfast, Liberty, and another sweet baby arriving soon. Once they started their families, Sunny would just be the ditzy sister and auntie who showed up occasionally, but didn't really contribute anything.

Now she didn't even have her art to hide behind.

Just her stupid smile.

"Bullshit!"

The shrieked word had her heart almost jumping out of her chest as she popped up and glanced around.

Something moved toward her through the water.

Something big and fast.

She couldn't help thinking of the scaly monster in the movie. She scrambled to get out of its way, but she wasn't fast enough and it plowed right into her, taking her down under in a tangle of . . . hard muscle and warm skin.

Chapter Four

AT FIRST, REID thought he'd run into a dead tree limb. But when the tree limb kicked at him, he realized his mistake. He grabbed the foot that came inches from his family jewels and surfaced to find . . .

"Sunshine." The word came out of his mouth like a curse. She didn't seem to take offense. She was too busy thrashing around and drowning.

He released her foot and hooked an arm around her waist, reeling her in. As soon as her body came in contact with his, he realized two things.

One, it had been way too long since he'd held a woman and he'd forgotten how damn good it felt.

And two, she was naked.

Sweet soft breasts melted against him, but it was the hard nipples drilling his chest that gave her state of clothing away.

His cock perked up and then jumped to full attention like a sleeping dog who had just gotten a whiff of a grilling T-bone steak.

Reid instantly released her and tried to swim away. Unfortunately, she had latched on to him like a life raft. Her hands clutched his shoulders while her legs were wrapped around his waist, her curvy ass brushing the top of his raging erection with each rippling wave.

There was a moment, one insane moment, when Reid actually thought about sliding his hands over that sweet ass and taking what his body so obviously wanted. She had made it clear that she wanted him. Even now, her moonlit eyes were filled with heat and a twinkle of excitement. He knew sex with her would be wild and exciting. And if anyone needed a little wild excitement, it was Reid. All his life he had chosen to walk the straight and narrow and look where it had gotten him.

He had no savings.

No woman.

And a belligerent teenager who hated his guts.

Of course, having sex with Sunny wasn't going to change any of those things. Even if he wanted a permanent relationship—which he didn't— Sunny wasn't the permanent relationship type. She was interested in him for one reason and one reason only. To entertain her while she was here. Once she grew bored with him, she would easily drop him like a hot potato. Or throw him under the bus with her brother.

Then he'd have no savings and no job.

Ignoring his body's demands, he leaned back and kicked toward the shallows. Once he could stand, he untangled her limbs from around him and headed for shore. He hoped she would continue her swim and leave him the hell alone.

He wasn't that lucky.

As soon as he grabbed his towel to dry off, he heard splashes behind him. He turned to see her walking out of the springs like a glorious, moonlit water nymph. He quickly turned back around, but not before the image of grapefruit-sized breasts topped with large rose-colored nipples was seared into his brain.

"So I guess you swim here often," she said.

He spotted her clothes lying on a nearby rock—something he wished he'd spotted earlier— and grabbed them, shoving them at her without turning. She laughed. She had one of those husky laughs that settled in a man's soul . . . and lower. He could still pound nails with the erection pressing against his wet swim trunks.

He needed to get out of there and he needed to get out of there now.

He picked up his boots and headed for the path that led to the trailer. He'd only taken a few steps when a sharp rock bit into his heel. Pain shot up his leg and had him cursing and hopping on one foot. Sunny's laughter made him even more hopping mad.

"The first rule of living on a ranch," she said in a smug voice. "Is never go outside without boots on. Something I thought an experienced cowboy would know."

He bit back the nasty retort on the tip of his tongue and sat down on a nearby rock to pull on his socks and boots. As he did, he couldn't help shooting a glance in Sunny's direction.

She wasn't naked. She wore a pair of panties

that were no more than a tiny scrap of turquoise material and a shorty shirt that didn't come close to covering her stomach. He couldn't help staring at the small sunflower tattooed just inside her hipbone, it's stem dipping beneath the elastic of her panties.

"I have a thing for sunflowers." Sunny's voice was soft and breathy. "You just can't help but smile when you see one."

Smiling wasn't what the sunflower made Reid want to do. It made him want to drop to his knees and lick each petal before his tongue followed the stem all the way down to the very tip. He wanted to blame his raging sexual need on the fact that he hadn't been with a woman since before his sister had called him. Which was almost a year ago. But while that didn't help matters, he knew most of the blame belonged on the sunflower-tattooed woman standing within reach.

Sunny was temptation incarnate. A sexy siren made to drive men wild.

If she hadn't been his boss's sister, Reid would have given in to that temptation. He would have licked her tattoo, worshiped her magnificent breasts with his mouth and hands, and then wrapped those long, tanned legs around his waist and driven so deep inside her he'd forget all about the way his vibrant, healthy sister had faded away to nothing but skin and bones. Forget he was a horrible guardian. Forget he'd lost the dream of owning his own ranch.

"So what kind of punishment did you give Sophie?"

Sunny's question pulled him from the path his brain had no business going down. He shook his head to clear it before he finished tugging on his boots. Without answering her question, he stood and headed down the path.

The trailer was parked just on the other side of the springs—a trailer that had been graciously offered to Reid by Sunny's brother. Reid needed to remember that. But it was hard to remember when Sunny kept pushing him.

A twig snapped behind him. Close behind him.

He stopped in his tracks and ran a hand through his hair in frustration. He had tried to keep his mouth shut in the hopes she would get the hint that he wasn't interested and leave him alone, but it looked like he was going to have to use words.

And he had never been good with words.

He turned to find Sunny standing there. She had put on a pair of jeans and turquoise boots that matched her panties. Her smile was bright and cheerful. Which just pissed him off even more.

"What's the matter with you? Can't you take a hint? It's none of your business how I disciplined Sophie. It's none of your business how often I come swimming. I don't know what you want from me, but you're not going to get it. I want nothing to do with a spoiled little rich girl who has nothing better to do with her life than spend her brother's money and follow men around like a dog in heat. So get the message, Sunshine Whitlock. I'm not interested!"

The smile stayed in place, but he could tell by the rigid way it froze on her face that he'd finally gotten through to her. He knew his words had been hurtful. But dammit, a man could only take so much temptation before he did something he would regret later.

He started walking again, but her shrieked cussword had him freezing in his tracks.

"Bullshit!"

He turned back around. Weirdly, she wasn't looking at him. She was staring up at a tree branch.

"It's not bullshit, Sunshine," he said. "My body might be interested, but I'm not. I need this job. I don't just need it for me. I need it for Sophie. After losing her mother, she needs the stability of a good home. So I would appreciate it if you didn't go running to your brother and have me fired for declining his little sister."

She pulled her gaze from the tree and stared at him. "That's what you think of me? You think I'm the type of woman who would get someone fired?" When he didn't say anything, she frowned. It was the first time he had ever seen her frown. Strangely, he liked it much better than her fake smile. "Well, you're wrong, Reid Mitchell. I'm not some spoiled little brat who runs to her brother every time someone doesn't like me. I'm a big girl who can deal with a little rejection. In fact, I've spent all my life dealing with it. So there's no need to worry about losing your job." She started to leave, but then stopped. "Oh, and by the way, I get the hint. I'll stay away from you. Far, far away." With a haughty sniff, she disappeared into the trees.

He should feel relieved.

So why didn't he?

Maybe because he didn't trust Sunny as far as he could throw her.

He didn't sleep well that night. If he wasn't worrying about getting fired, he was thinking about cradling moonlit breasts in his hands and following tattooed sunflower stems with his tongue. Once he pushed those thoughts from his mind, his guilt kicked in and he started feeling badly about being so harsh with her. What had she meant about it not being the first time she'd been rejected? No man in his right mind would reject a woman who looked like Sunny. The only reason he had was his job.

A job he still might lose.

Since he ended up only getting a few hours sleep, he was in a foul mood the following morning. It didn't help that Sophie was still pouting about him confiscating her cellphone for taking his truck without permission. She glared at him across the kitchen table the entire time she ate her bowl of Cinnamon Toast Crunch, crunching so loudly he wanted to pull out his hair.

On the way to take her to school, he tried to think up some wise parental words to explain why he'd taken her phone. But nothing came to mind. So all she received when she got out of the truck was a mumbled, "Have a good day," before he pulled away.

When he reached the Holiday Ranch, he

wouldn't have been surprised to find Corbin waiting to fire him. But the only people sitting on the porch were Hallie and her grandmother, Mimi. Neither one of them looked like they were the bearers of bad news.

Of course, Corbin could arrive at any second.

"Come on up, Reid," Hallie called as soon as he got out of his truck. "Mama made cinnamon rolls and they're still warm."

He wasted no time heading up the porch steps. If he were going to be canned, he'd rather leave with his stomach full of Darla Holiday's delicious cinnamon rolls. As soon as Hallie handed him a plate, he dug in to the yeasty rolls covered in brown sugar, cinnamon, and thick white icing.

Mimi chuckled. "I do love a man with a good appetite."

Mimi Holiday was a piece of work. She had been just as welcoming as the rest of the Holidays, but there was a calculating gleam in her eyes that always made Reid feel a little leery. Not to mention, she didn't believe in beating around the bush.

Once Reid finished the cinnamon roll, she sent him a pointed look. "I hear your niece stole your truck and took it for a joyride."

"Mimi!" Hallie said.

Mimi glanced at her granddaughter. "What? If it was a secret, you should have said so." She looked back at Reid. "And it's not like other parents haven't had to deal with the same thing. Three of my granddaughters stole Hank's truck without permission. Hallie here included."

Hallie turned to her. "You knew? But I never told anyone. Not even my sisters."

Mimi shrugged. "It's called being older and wiser . . . and a bit of an insomniac. I watched you from my bedroom window."

"Why didn't you tell Daddy?"

"Because all you did was drive around in circles in the back pasture. And I knew why you did it. You were ticked off at your daddy and needed to blow off some steam. There's no harm in that." She looked at Reid. "But there is harm in what Sophie did. Sunny could have been seriously hurt . . . or even killed when Sophie ran her off the road."

Reid wiped his mouth with a napkin. "You mean when Sunny ran Sophie off the road."

Hallie sent her grandmother a warning look, but Mimi didn't even glance in her direction. "That's not what I mean at all. According to what Sunny told my granddaughters in their Secret Sisterhood meeting, it was Sophie who ran Sunny off the road. Sunny just took the blame so Sophie wouldn't get into trouble. And if it had just been a little joyride like Hallie took, I would agree. But looking at your phone while driving on a highway is not just a little joyride. It's dangerous. As Sophie's guardian, you need to know about it so you can make sure it doesn't happen again."

Reid looked at Hallie. "She was on her phone?"

Hallie sighed and nodded. "At least that's what Sophie told Sunny."

Reid didn't know whom he was most mad at. Sophie or Sunny. Probably Sunny. Most kids would come up with a lie to get out of trouble. Sunny was an adult and he didn't doubt for a second she was the one who had concocted the cock-and-bull story about hydroplaning and running off the road.

He jumped to his feet. "If you'll excuse me, I need to talk with Sunny and get the information straight from the horse's mouth." But before he could turn to leave, Mimi pointed a finger at him.

"Sit down!"

He sat back down.

"You don't need to go running over to Corbin's with both guns blazing," Mimi said. "That's a sure way to get yourself fired. Corbin likes you a lot, but he adores his little sister and can't see past the end of his nose where she's concerned."

"Mimi's right," Hallie said. "Besides, Sunny only lied because she was trying to protect Sophie."

"From her own flesh and blood!" he snapped. "What did she think I was going to do? Beat my own niece black and blue?"

"Maybe she has reason to believe that's how guardians deal with ornery teenagers," Mimi said. Before Reid could ask what she meant, she continued. "But Sunny's not the problem. Sophie is. She's mourning her mama and having to deal with a new school and a new parent. That would be too much for anyone, let alone a fifteen-year-old girl."

Reid knew that. He just didn't know how to help her.

Mimi reached out and squeezed his hand. "I know it's not easy balancing discipline with love and understanding, but you'll figure it out. And if you need help, you just say the word." She winked. "I'm a bit of an expert on dealing with teenage girls."

There was a part of him that wanted to take Mimi up on the offer, but the other part—the stubborn part—refused to let his bosses think he couldn't handle his own family matters.

He got up and pulled on his hat. "Thanks, Ms. Mimi, but I got things taken care of."

The first thing he was going to take care of was giving Sunshine Whitlock a piece of his mind.

Chapter Five

Sunny wasn't surprised to wake up to full sunlight streaming across her bed. After she'd gotten back from Cooper Springs, she had tossed and turned until close to five o'clock in the morning . . . with Reid's harsh words circling around and around in her head. Even as she blinked awake, the names he'd called her were still there.

Spoiled little rich girl.

Dog in heat.

What made them even worse was she couldn't deny them. She was a spoiled little rich girl and she had been trailing after Reid like a dog in heat. There was something about the man that made her do things she had never done in her life. She wasn't a saint by any means, but she had never been so blatant about her sexual interest. In fact, she had never had to pursue a man. They'd always pursued her. If she showed any interest, they were more than happy to oblige.

Every man but Reid.

He wanted nothing to do with her. Even though it had been quite obvious he'd liked what he'd seen. Not only had she felt his impressive erection, she'd also seen it pressing against the front of his swimsuit. Unfortunately, his body might like her, but his brain didn't.

Probably because she *was* a spoiled little rich girl.

It hadn't always been true. While her and Corbin's parents hadn't been dirt poor, they'd lived from paycheck to paycheck. Usually separately. Mama and Daddy had a tumultuous marriage. They couldn't go for more than a few months without getting into a fight that sent one or the other packing. When that happened, Corbin and Sunny had been pawned off on whatever relative was willing to take them. They had lived with grandmas, aunts, uncles, and cousins. None of them had a lot of money . . . especially that they wanted to share with two orphaned relatives. She and Corbin had spent their lives wearing hand-me-down clothes and shoes and never asking for more than what they were given.

It wasn't until Corbin had gotten old enough to get his own job that Sunny had gotten her first pair of name-brand athletic shoes. She had been over the moon and Corbin had been thrilled he could make her happy.

Looking back, that's how it had all started—Corbin enjoying buying her things and her enjoying getting them. As they grew, the gifts got more and more extravagant. She went from designer sneakers to expensive jewelry, cars, vacations, and an apartment in Paris so she could study art. Corbin had even bought her the Holiday Ranch.

It was the only gift she hadn't accepted and not because she hadn't wanted it. As a kid, she had dreamed about living on the Holiday Ranch as much as she had dreamed about being one of the Holiday sisters. But she hadn't been able to allow Mimi, Darla, and Hank to be thrown out of their family home. So she had convinced Corbin she really didn't want the ranch and had run off to Houston.

But it was still Corbin's money that paid for the apartment she lived in. Still, his money that bought her car, her clothes, and her food. She tried to act like she was making it as an artist, but the truth was she couldn't pay her cellphone bill with the money she made off her paintings. She hadn't sold one painting in the last three months and Corbin had made sure she'd had plenty of gallery showings.

A newspaper art critic had summed it up.

S. B. Whitlock has skills . . . just no talent.

In other words, Sunny was just a talentless, spoiled rich girl.

As she lay there, she grew more and more depressed . . . and more and more anxious. If she had been in Houston, she would have chosen some thrill-seeking thing to do—skydiving or wakeboarding or driving a race car at the motorsport track. The city offered numerous adrenaline-pumping activities. But here in Wilder, there was nothing but skinny-dipping at

Cooper's Springs and that was the cause of her anxiety.

Which left only one thing.

Getting up, she quickly dressed in an old T-shirt, jeans, and boots. Corbin and Belle had left two of her favorite Strawberry Sweet Cakes muffins from Nothin' But Muffins and a note on the kitchen table saying they'd gone into town and would be back later. Sunny grabbed one of the muffins and a bottle of water from the refrigerator before she set out for the Holiday Ranch.

It was a glorious spring day. The midday sun shone brightly, but a cool breeze kept the temperature from being too hot. Bluebonnets were in full bloom and the pastures looked like a purplish-blue sea that rippled in the breeze. If Sunny had been in a better mood, she might have stopped to enjoy the sight. Instead, she barely paid attention as she headed toward the Holidays' farmhouse.

When she got there, she spotted Mimi working in her garden. Sunny loved the older woman. Mimi was the type of grandma Sunny had always wished for—a kind yet strong woman who loved her family above all else. Normally, Sunny would make a beeline straight for Mimi and help her with her gardening. Today, she was too anxious to be around people. So she merely smiled and waved before heading up the porch steps.

As soon as she entered, she could hear Darla working in the kitchen. The sisters' mama was an excellent cook and was always in the kitchen preparing food for her large family. Darla, Hank,

Mimi, Hallie, and Jace might be the only ones living in the farmhouse, but the other married sisters and their families stopped by often.

Bypassing the kitchen, Sunny took the stairs to the second level. Once there, she walked to the end of the hallway where the dropdown stairs that led to the attic were located.

The short time Sunny had lived at the ranch, the attic had become her place to paint. With Mimi's and Darla's help, she had cleared out an entire area right by one of the big dormer windows and turned it into an art studio.

When she lived there, Sunny had spent hours painting the idyllic country scenes just outside the windows. Country landscapes were her specialty. Or had been before all the bad reviews had given her painter's block. Now she couldn't even paint a plain slat fence that didn't look like a kindergartener's.

But today, she didn't want to paint fences or idyllic country scenes.

Today, her anxiety pushed her to paint something darker . . . something angrier.

After adjusting her easel, she took the largest canvas from the stack leaning against the wall and placed it on the bottom canvas holder before securing it with the top holder. Moving to her art table, she went through the wide array of acrylic paints. After selecting Prussian green, cobalt blue, and raw sienna, she squirted some of each in plastic Solo cups before adding glazing liquid and water from a jug she kept on the table. Once the paint was thinned and mixed to the desired consistency, she picked up the container of green paint and moved over to the easel.

She studied the pristine white canvas for only a moment before she lifted the cup and with a snap of her wrist . . . threw the paint at it.

It landed in a satisfying splat. She watched the paint drip down the canvas before she continued splattering paint until the cup was empty. Then she did the same with the blue and brown paint until the canvas was completely covered with dripping splats of paint.

She stood back and studied it. It was a true mess, but there was something missing. Mainly, her anxiety. After tossing the paint cups in the trash, she squirted some scarlet-red paint onto a palette, mixed it with a little burnt umber, then scooped some onto a long, thin palette knife and started applying the red to the splattered painting. The more she streaked globs of red through the dripping splats the more the tight knot of anxiety in her gut loosened.

She layered in other colors using her palette knife, mars black and ultramarine blue, before she picked up a brush and start adding highlights and shadows. She worked until her arm ached and her back hurt. When she was finally finished, she stood back and studied the painting.

She laughed. "If the art critics would see this, they'd really think I don't have any talent."

Thankfully, no one would ever see it. Once it had dried, Sunny would hide it with the other angry art that was stacked under a tarp in the corner of the attic. She should probably start throwing the paintings away—not only the ones here, but also the ones she'd painted in Houston. Maybe, if she ever had the courage to tell the Holiday sisters about her strange violent art, they could have a big bonfire and burn all of them.

And all her pent up anger with them.

"Sunny?"

She startled and glanced at the opening to the attic just as Mimi's white head appeared.

"Hey, Mimi!" She quickly turned the easel to the wall. "No need to come up. I'll come down."

Of course, Mimi didn't listen. She never listened.

She finished climbing the stairs. "You okay? You've been up here for hours."

Hours?

Sunny glanced out the window, surprised to see that the bright midday light had changed to shadowy dusk. "Goodness. I didn't realize how late it was getting. I was going to help you garden."

"No worries. There are plenty of days left to get the garden ready for planting. You need to get on home." Mimi glanced at Sunny's paint-splattered clothes. "And get washed up. Corbin called looking for you. I guess he's taking you and Belle out to dinner at the Hellhole tonight."

Sunny grabbed a rag to wipe off her hands. She felt much better than she had earlier, but she still didn't feel like going out. Or maybe what she didn't feel like was running into Reid.

"I might just pass on dinner," she said.

Mimi studied her. "Something wrong?"

She shook her head. "No. I'm fine. I just feel a little tired, is all."

"I can understand why. Getting into an accident can sure knock the wind out of you."

Sunny blinked. "An accident?"

Mimi scowled. "So you're going to lie to me like you did to Corbin?"

"Umm . . . I . . . who told you?"

"Hallie."

So much for thinking that what was discussed at the Secret Sisterhood meetings was sacred. Or maybe that rule only applied to real sisters.

Sunny sighed. "Did you tell Corbin?"

"No, but I'm sure Belle did. Wives don't usually keep things from their husbands. I'm sure all the husbands know by now . . . along with Reid Mitchell."

"Reid? Hallie told Reid?"

"I told Reid. As Sophie's guardian, he needed to know."

Sunny flopped down on a nearby trunk. "Great. Now Reid will really hate me."

Mimi took a seat on a trunk across from her. "I don't think he hates you. He was a little upset when he learned the truth, but I'm sure by now he's had some time to think about it and realizes you only did it to protect Sophie."

Sunny didn't think he'd see it that way.

"He's a good man, that one," Mimi continued. "The way he took on his niece after his sister passed away proves it. Not many single men would be willing to take on a belligerent teenager. Still, I can tell that he's questioning his decision. And like most men, he's too stubborn to admit he needs help."

Sunny snorted. "Stubborn and mean spirited."

Mimi studied her. "So you aren't like the other single women in town who are drooling over him?"

"Not hardly." When Mimi lifted her eyebrows, Sunny quickly amended, "I mean he's good looking and all, but I like my men to smile more than once every ten years."

Mimi laughed. "He is a solemn man. But have you ever heard the saying, 'Still waters run deep'? I think there's a lot more to Reid than his stubbornness and solemn personality." A twinkle entered her eyes. A twinkle Sunny had seen before when Mimi was up to something. "It will just take the right woman to dig deep enough to find it."

Sunny's eyes widened. "I hope you're not getting any ideas that I'm the right woman, Mimi. Reid can barely tolerate me and I'm not real partial to him either." At least, she wasn't after finding out he thought she was a spoiled brat. "And even if I was, it wouldn't work out when I live in Houston."

The twinkle got even brighter before she looked away. "Well, you're probably right." She stood. "But that doesn't mean you can't enjoy other good-lookin' Wilder men. Now get on home and get cleaned up. Young women shouldn't be hiding away in an attic when they can be kicking up their heels at the Hellhole."

After she was gone, Sunny moved back to the

paint table to clean up. While she was closing up tubes of paint, she glanced out the window and saw a horse and rider crossing the pasture behind the barn. She didn't need to see the face beneath the brown Stetson to know who it was.

She wanted to look away, but her eyes didn't obey her brain. She continued to watch as Reid approached. As he got closer, she could see the way he sat a saddle. Comfortable. Easy. Like he'd been riding every day of his life. His body moved as one with the horse, his hand loosely holding the reins as if he didn't even need them to guide the horse. Once he came around the barn, she got a view from the back.

It must have been a hard day on the range because sweat stuck his western shirt to his broad shoulders and his dark hair to his strong-corded neck. Sunny's fingers twitched with the need to run through those damp strands. She fisted her hand and continued to watch as he swung down from the saddle in one fluid move that made her heart skip a beat. It skipped again when he froze and his head slowly turned in her direction and tipped up.

She jumped back from the window, squirting the red paint she held all over her shirt. She stared down at the mess and cursed. What was she doing? The man had told her to stay away from him and here she was mooning over him like an infatuated fool. Well, she might be an untalented, spoiled rich girl, but she was no fool.

Mimi was right.

Just because an arrogant cowboy had hurt her

feelings that didn't mean she should hide away in an attic.

Reid Mitchell wasn't the only handsome cowboy in Wilder, Texas.

Chapter Six

UNFORTUNATELY, SUNNY DIDN'T end up dancing the night away with some hot cowboy. As soon as they got into town, Corbin took the turnoff to the Holiday Bed and Breakfast.

"I thought we were going to the Hellhole for dinner," Sunny said.

Corbin, who sat in the driver's seat in front of her, lifted his shoulders in a shrug. "We have to stop off at the bed-and-breakfast to pick up Liberty and Jesse."

Sunny didn't understand why Liberty and Jesse weren't just meeting them at the restaurant, especially when Jesse loved driving his big ol' monster truck with his wife tucked against his side. Sunny grew even more confused when she saw the line of cars parked along the road leading to the big mansion Jesse had bought and renovated. The bed-and-breakfast hadn't opened yet, and even if it had, there weren't enough rooms to accommodate this many people.

She was about to ask what was going on when

Corbin pulled in front of the house and she saw the banner hanging between the columns.

Happy Birthday, Sunny!

A second later, the front door opened and what looked like half the town spilled out, yelling, "Surprise!"

Sunny was stunned. "But my birthday isn't until next month."

Corbin got out and opened her door with a big smile on his face. "Believe me, I know when your birthday is, Sunshine Brook. You start reminding me weeks before. Which is why I had Belle and Libby plan the party so early. For once, I wanted you to be surprised."

So that's why the sisters were acting so strange.

Tears filled her eyes and she dove into his arms. "I am surprised. Thank you, Cory!"

He drew back and smiled. "Anything for my little sister. And don't thank me. Thank Libby and Belle. They did all the work."

She turned to Belle who had come around to their side. "I don't know what to say, Belly."

Belle hugged her close. "You don't need to say anything. That's what sisters do. Although I thought for sure Noelle had given it away last night when she said she'd see you tonight."

"Sorry." Noelle appeared with the rest of the sisters. "I've never been good at keeping secrets."

Sunny laughed. "And here I thought y'all were having a meeting without me."

"Never." Sweetie tugged her close. "You're part of us now."

While Sunny's heart swelled in her chest, all the

sisters took turns giving her a hug before Noelle and Belle hooked her arms and led her toward the crowd of people waiting to wish her a happy birthday. Once she made it through them, Jesse stood at the door, waiting to welcome her inside with a big smile and a wink.

"Happy Early Birthday, sis!"

As soon as she stepped inside, Sunny let out a gasp. The entire lower floor had been decorated in her favorite color: yellow. There were clusters of yellow balloons, festoons of ribbon and streamers, and vases of daffodils and daisies and sunflowers. The buffet set up in the large dining room included all of Sunny's favorite foods: sausage and jalapeno pizza, spicy chicken wings, and Tito's chorizo tacos. The dessert table was filled with three-tiered dessert trays of Strawberry Sweet Cake muffins, lemon bars, and fudgy brownies with pecan ganache frosting. In the very center of the table was a large sheet cake decorated like a sunflower.

Sunny was overwhelmed

Almost too overwhelmed.

She didn't deserve all this. She didn't deserve even half of this. Not when she had lied to everyone about how well her paintings were selling. She felt even worse when Jesse spoke.

"This isn't just a birthday celebration, you know. This is also to celebrate your success in the art world and all your hard work."

"And the surprises aren't over yet." Corbin drew her close and kissed the side of her head.

"Jesse and I still have two surprises we think you're going to love."

Jesse rubbed his hands together. "But right now, let's eat. I'm starving!"

With the hard knot of guilt sitting in her stomach, Sunny wasn't hungry. But she filled a plate anyway and pretended to eat as she walked around and chatted with the townsfolk and thanked them for coming. As soon as no one was looking, she dumped the full plate of food into the trash.

Unfortunately, someone was watching.

"Seems like a waste of good food."

She whirled around to see Mrs. Stokes standing there in a vintage designer suit and ratty mink stole. Mrs. Stokes was the wealthiest woman in Wilder and the town matriarch. While Sunny admired her, Mrs. Stokes also intimidated her. No doubt because she was a strong, successful woman while Sunny was weak and an utter failure.

"Oh, hey, Ms. Stokes," she said. "I guess my eyes were bigger than my stomach."

Mrs. Stokes studied her. "Or maybe it's hard to eat when you're the guest of honor. I had the same problem when my fourth husband threw me a surprise party." No one in town seemed to know how many times Mrs. Stokes had been married and she didn't seem to know either. "No wait, Buford was my third husband." She shook her head. "Anyway, Buford went all out. He invited the entire town and had it catered with more food than we had at our wedding. But I was too overwhelmed by all the love to eat a thing. Maybe that's why poor Buford ate enough for both of us. He died from a heart attack that very night. After that, I made my husbands and boyfriends swear to never throw me a surprise party again."

She reached in the pocket of her stole and pulled out a package of gum. Mrs. Stokes had been a chain smoker until she had made a deal with Corbin to quit. She had gone from chewing nicotine gum to chewing Wrigley's spearmint that Corbin bought for her by the case on Amazon. No one knew exactly what their deal was and Sunny had bugged Corbin relentlessly to no avail.

Once Mrs. Stokes unwrapped a stick and popped it into her mouth, she offered some to Sunny. When she declined, Mrs. Stokes stuck the package back in the mink's inside pocket. "I don't much care for gum either, but you do what you have to do to get what you want."

Again, Sunny wondered what it was Mrs. Stokes wanted so badly she was willing to give up her beloved cigarettes. She might have asked if the old woman's gaze hadn't zeroed in on something—or someone—behind Sunny.

"I wonder what has that good-looking cowboy staring so intently in our direction. Let's hope he has a thing for older women."

Sunny turned and was instantly caught in a pair of champagne-colored eyes. Except they weren't sparkling with effervescence. They were bubbling with anger. She knew exactly why he was so mad ... and at whom. She wanted to turn back around and pretend like she hadn't seen him, but Mrs. Stokes made it impossible.

"Well, don't just stand there gawkin', Reid Mitchell. Get over here and say hello."

Reid moved up next to Sunny, making her wish she'd worn heels instead of flats. At five eight, she wasn't short by any means, and yet, Reid seemed to tower over her. "Good evenin', Ms. Stokes. How are you enjoying the party?"

"Better than it looks like you are. What has you looking fit to be tied? Did your favorite dog run off?"

"I don't own a dog, ma'am."

"Well, maybe that's your problem." Mrs. Stokes turned to the two women standing by the refreshment table chatting. Sheryl Ann ran Nothin' But Muffins with Noelle, and Melba worked at the sheriff's office and fostered abused and orphaned animals. "Melba! We got someone here in need of a pet."

Sunny choked back a laugh as Reid stared in horror at Mrs. Stokes. "No, Ms. Stokes, I don't need—"

Mrs. Stokes cut him off. "Well, if you don't, that cute little niece of yours does. Maybe if she had a pet, she wouldn't be stealing trucks and running people off the road."

Reid shot a mean glare at Sunny as Melba came hustling up looking like she'd just won the lottery. "Someone needs a pet?"

Mrs. Stokes pointed at Reid. "Reid here."

"I don't need—"

This time, Melba cut him off. "I have a terrier

mix I call Faith Hill. And Patsy Cline, the cutest little lop-eared rabbit you've ever seen."

"A rabbit?" Sophie came up. Once again, the teenager looked like she'd gotten into her mother's makeup drawer without permission. "I love rabbits!"

Reid shook his head. "No rabbit, Soph."

Sophie sent Reid the same glare he had just sent Sunny before she whirled and stomped off.

"Oops," Mrs. Stokes said. "I didn't mean to cause a family tiff. I just thought a pet might help out a young girl who's obviously grieving."

Melba sent Reid a hopeful look. "Patsy really is a sweetheart. She uses a litter box and loves to cuddle and is a spry little thing—even though she's missing a foot."

Sunny's heart broke. "She's missing a foot? What happened?"

"The shelter I got her from didn't know. But with the clean cut, they think it's possible that someone just wanted a lucky rabbit's foot."

"That's horrible. The poor thing."

Melba's eyes lit up. "She would make a great pet for an artist."

Sunny had never owned a pet in her life and not because she didn't love animals. She adored animals. Adored them so much, she didn't want to saddle them with an irresponsible pet owner who couldn't stay in one place for longer than a few months. Like kids, pets should have a stable home. Sunny's life was about the furthest thing from stable. She refused to be like her parents and take on responsibilities she couldn't handle.

"I'm sorry, Melba, but my apartment in Houston doesn't allow pets."

Melba didn't look at all disappointed. In fact, she winked. "That's the one thing about life . . . things change when you least expect it. Now I think I'll go help myself to one of those lemon bars."

"That sounds like a good idea, Mel," Mrs. Stokes said. "I think I'll join you."

Once the two ladies were gone, Sunny was stuck with grumpy Reid who looked like he had eaten an entire tree of lemons. She had hoped to avoid him, but now she figured it was best to let him get all his anger out.

"Well, go ahead. Let me have it."

Those champagne eyes narrowed on her and he leaned in close, causing desire to zing through her body like a pinball lighting up all her erroneous zones.

What was the matter with her? Why did this grumpy, annoying man turn her into a limp noodle of lust?

The lust only grew when he spoke in a sexy, raspy voice. "Oh, I'd love nothing more than to let you have it." *Let me have it. Please let me have it.* "You had no business teaching Sophie that lying was the best way to get out of trouble. Unfortunately, I can't tell you exactly what I think of you without becoming the topic of gossip at Nothin' But Muffins—'Did you hear about how big bad Reid Mitchell made sweet Sunny Whitlock boohoo at her surprise birthday party?'"

She tried to ignore the virile scent of horses

and leather that wafted from his body like the most potent aphrodisiac. "Boohooing is not really my thing."

He studied her. This close, she could see the different shades of gold and brown that contributed to the unique champagne color of his eyes. She knew if she mixed dozens of colors of paint, she would never get this color exactly right. "Is that why you didn't go running to your brother and tell him about what happened at Cooper Springs? Or are you saving that piece of information to blackmail me with later?"

The man certainly knew how to get emotions out of her. Anger flooded her, erasing all traces of lust. Sunny had never wanted to physically harm anyone in her life, but she wanted to harm this man. She wanted to punch the smug look off his face with her fist.

And she couldn't. Not when the entire town watched.

She pinned on a smile and spoke through her teeth. "As much as you think I'm the devil, I have no intentions of telling anyone about what happened last night at Cooper Springs. Although whoever was eavesdropping on our conversation might."

"What are you talking about? Someone else was there last night?"

"You didn't hear them yell out 'bullshit'?"

His eyes narrowed. "What game are you playing? That was you."

"Nope. Someone was hiding in the trees."

He looked confused. "Why didn't you say anything?"

"Because you were too busy telling me what a spoiled little rich girl I am and how you want nothing to do with me." She should have left it at that and walked away, but she just couldn't do it. "Funny, but that's not what your body said when we were snuggled like two peas in a pod in Cooper Springs." She stepped closer and rested her hand on his chest. Beneath the starched fabric of his shirt, she felt his pectoral muscle jump and flex. When she lifted her gaze, his eyes swirled with something that made her breath catch.

Desire. Definitely, desire . . . mixed with a heavy dose of anger.

"People can't always control their bodily reactions," he growled.

He had a good point. Sunny felt like she'd downed an entire bottle of tequila—all flushed and woozy. That was just from touching his chest. What would it feel like to run her hand up his strong neck and cradle that sexy stubbled jaw? To lean up on her toes and press her lips to the stern line of his—

"Sunny!"

She stepped away from Reid just as Jesse appeared.

"Come on, sis!" Jesse took her hand that still tingled from Reid's heat. "It's time for presents."

She gave those heated champagne eyes one more glance before she allowed Jesse to lead her away.

She expected her brother to lead her into the

parlor or library to unwrap her presents and was confused when he led her up the stairs to the second floor. And even more confused when everyone at the party followed behind them with big smiles on their faces. When they got to the second floor, they walked past all the bedrooms that were named for the Holiday sisters: The Sweetheart Room, the Clover Room, the Liberty Room, the Belle Room, the Halloween Room, and the Noelle Room. At the very end of the hall was the door that led to the attic. Next to it was another nameplate.

Sunshine Room.

She turned to Jesse. "I get my own room?"

He laughed. "Of course you get your own room. You're my sister."

She squealed and hugged him tight before drawing back. "Is it ready? Can I see it?"

He opened the door and waved a hand to the narrow staircase. "Go right ahead."

She didn't need to be told twice. She raced up the stairs and let out another squeal when she saw her room. It was even bigger than the Holidays' attic with six large dormer windows she knew would let in tons of light during the day.

Modern blinds were lowered below puffy canary-yellow valances. The walls were a lighter shade of lemon yellow and trimmed in white. The bed was big and shiny brass with a white duvet and pillow shams and a half dozen throw pillows in different prints: stripes, sunflowers, and cute buzzing bees. The same palette of yellows carried through to the en suite bathroom with the tiled shower and freestanding soaker tub.

"Oh my gosh," she said as she peeked into the huge walk-in closet. "It's awesome."

"You haven't seen the best part." Jesse pulled her out of the closet and pointed to the other side of the room.

It had been turned into a painting studio. An easel was set up by the windows and empty canvases were lined up in a wooden holder on the back wall—along with a deep sink and long counter with plenty of shelves above for paints and supplies.

"Well?" Jesse said. "What do you think?"

She thought she needed to tell her family that she was a complete failure. But how could she do it when Jesse, Corbin, and all the Holidays were crowded into the room with huge smiles and love shining in their eyes?

"It's perfect," she whispered. "Just perfect." She glanced at the studio. "But do you think the art studio was a good idea? I mean I'll love it when I come to visit, but your guests might not."

Jesse exchanged looks with Corbin. "I'm sure we'll figure it out. For now, Corbin wants to give you your present and folks are dying to get a peek at the Sunshine Room." He winked. "Who knows? Maybe the townsfolk have relatives who would love to stay in an artist's loft."

Something wasn't right. Even if people wanted to stay in an artist loft, why the huge closet? People staying for a few nights or even a week didn't need a walk-in closet. Or all the space. Jesse could have made two rooms out of the attic and they both would have been plenty big. Even she knew that would have made more business sense. Jesse was a businessman who hadn't made a bad investment decision in his life.

What was going on?

As it turned out, she didn't have to wait long to find out.

As soon as Corbin led her out back to the carriage house, all the pieces fell into place.

When Jesse had first bought the house, he'd renovated the carriage house for Belle and Liberty's event-planning business, Holiday Sisters Events. The upper floor housed their offices and the lower half was storage for their event supplies. But the storage warehouse was so large that Liberty and Belle had only filled half of it with catering supplies and decorations. The other half had been empty space.

Until now.

Now it had been turned into a storefront with a huge picture window and glass door. Through that window and door, Sunny could see the beautifully lit space inside ... a gallery space with plenty of blank white walls for art. Before she even lifted her gaze to the sign above the door, she knew what she'd find.

S. B. Whitlock Gallery

Corbin had built her a gallery ... for all her paintings no one wanted.

Chapter Seven

Reid woke with a nagging headache. He hoped a hot shower would help, but Sophie had used all the hot water. After his ice-cold shower, he couldn't find a clean pair of underwear. He headed to the laundry room where he found his dirty clothes piled up on the floor in a heap. He tossed them all in the washer with a couple detergent pods and started it before he went to his room and scavenged around until he found a holey pair of underwear.

Once dressed, he went in search of Sophie. He found her sitting at the kitchen table, spooning cereal into her mouth as she scratched out math problems in a notebook. Since the day had started out so badly, he thought about just ignoring the laundry situation. But a good parent wouldn't do that.

He leaned against the counter and crossed his arms. "Look, Soph, I know you're mad at me for taking your phone, but that doesn't mean you get to shirk your chores. We agreed that I'd clean the bathroom and vacuum and you would dust and do the laundry. So make sure you get those chores done when you get home from school." He glanced down at the notebook. "After you finish all your homework. Homework shouldn't be rushed through at breakfast."

He wasn't surprised she completely ignored him. She had been giving him the silent treatment since last night's party. He didn't know if it had to do with him refusing to give back her cellphone for two more weeks after finding out about her texting and driving or not letting her have a rabbit.

Probably both.

When she continued writing out equations, he sighed. "Finish up so I can get you to school."

She continued the silent treatment on the way to school. Which left him to his own thoughts. Or one thought. One thought that had plagued him since the party.

He wanted Sunny Whitlock.

He wanted her in a bad way.

All she'd had to do was touch him and he'd ignited like dry prairie grass struck by lightning. He knew she had been trying to prove a point. He also knew she had felt the sexual attraction too. There had been a moment when he thought she was going to kiss him.

And he'd wanted her to.

Which was dangerous.

She was a seductress he needed to stay away from if he wanted to keep his job.

Although, last night, she hadn't looked like a seductress. She'd looked like a sweet country girl in the modest yellow sundress that fell to her knees and cute little yellow sandals. Half of her strawberry-blond hair had been twisted up in a pile of curls and the rest fell around her shoulders in soft waves. The only makeup she'd worn was the softest pink lipstick he'd ever seen. He'd tossed and turned all night thinking about what he wanted to do to that soft pink mouth ... what he wanted it to do to him.

Those weren't the only thoughts that had plagued him.

He hadn't followed the crowd upstairs to see the room Jesse had renovated for his sister. Instead, he had slipped outside to cool off. So he was there when the entire party had moved outside. Standing in the shadows, he'd been able to watch Sunny's expression when she realized Corbin had renovated half the carriage house into a gallery for her. Her expression hadn't been that of a woman overjoyed with a gift.

She had looked overwhelmingly sad before she'd pinned on a smile and squealed with happiness. Reid couldn't figure out why. If someone gifted him a ranch, he would be ... ticked off he hadn't earned it himself.

And maybe that was why Sunny had looked so upset. Although that was doubtful. She hadn't had to work for anything in her life and she wasn't about to start now. She probably just didn't think the gallery was big enough or the sign glitzy enough. And what was he doing wasting his time thinking about it? He didn't need to be thinking about Sunny. He had other problems.

Mainly, the one sitting in the passenger seat.

He glanced over at Sophie and made another effort to end her silence. "So what did you think of the party? Pretty extravagant, huh? I mean who spends that much money on flowers and decorations that you're just going to throw away?" He shook his head. "What a waste. No wonder Sunny is a spoiled brat. Her family, obviously, doesn't understand the value of money."

Faster than he could blink, Sophie whirled on him. "Decorations and flowers are never a waste! They make things pretty. But you wouldn't know anything about that because you don't like pretty things. Which is why you don't like Sunny . . . and why you never liked my mama!"

Reid stared at her in shock. This was what he got for trying to talk to her. "I loved your mama. She was my sister."

"No, you didn't. If you had loved her, you would have helped her when she needed help."

He tried to tamp down his temper, but it was impossible after everything he had done for Bree. "You don't think I helped your mama? In case you don't remember, I was the only one there helping the last few months of her life."

"I'm not talking about you coming after she was already dying. You did that out of guilt—because you wouldn't have been able to keep your holier-than-thou image if you hadn't. But that's not love. If you had loved her, you wouldn't have let her leave home in the first place."

"I was a kid when she left, Soph. There's no way I could have stopped her."

"Did you even try?"

When he didn't reply quick enough, she snorted. "That's what I thought. And news flash, you weren't a kid when she got pregnant with me or when she was a young mother struggling to make ends meet. But you still didn't call or come to see us once. Not once!"

He waited until he had pulled into the drop-off lane at the high school before he turned to her. "It was her choice to leave, Soph. No one made her. And she could have come home anytime she wanted. She chose not to."

"Because she didn't feel like you wanted her! She didn't feel like you and Grandma cared. And you didn't care. You didn't care about her at all. You didn't even care that she got cancer and died. You just cared that it inconvenienced you—that it's still inconveniencing you. But you don't have to worry. As soon as I can, I plan to stop inconveniencing you." She jerked open the door of the truck and jumped out, slamming it hard behind her.

He started to open his door to go after her, but then stopped. Go after her and say what? That she wasn't an inconvenience. She'd read through the lie as easily as she had read his mind. He did feel inconvenienced. And who wouldn't when their sister called out of nowhere and dropped a huge burden on them?

Except it wasn't the burden's fault.

But somehow Reid had blamed Sophie anyway.

A cacophony of horn honking made him realize that he had brought the drop-off line to a complete standstill. He inched up and slowly followed the line out of the parking lot. He needed to get back to the ranch. He and Hallie had planned to check out the spring calves and make any changes they needed for the next breeding season. But his mind was racing so much he didn't think he could plan anything.

What did Sophie mean when she'd said she was going to stop inconveniencing him? Was she going to run off like her mother had? Or maybe do something worse? He knew kids committed suicide, but surely Sophie wasn't talking about that.

Was she?

A series of pings drew his attention to the glove box where he'd stashed Sophie's phone when he had confiscated it. After what she had just said, he couldn't help flipping it open and taking the cellphone out. A line of texts filled the screen.

Texts from someone named JC.

Where r u?

Still on for 2nite at Cooper Springs?

Got the johnnies so NP.

Reid was trying to figure out what the text meant when a horn blared.

This time, it wasn't behind him.

It was in front of him.

As he was looking at the phone, he must have veered over into the opposite lane and was now heading straight for a big monster truck.

"Shit!" He swerved back into his lane before they hit, then watched with sick horror in his side mirror as the truck swerved off the road and crushed an entire row of weeds before coming to a dust-spitting stop.

Reid made a quick U-turn and pulled up behind the truck. He knew the vehicle. Everyone in town knew the big-assed truck with its monster tires, faded bumper stickers, and Texas and American flags hanging from poles situated on either side of the chrome roll bar.

He jumped out, ready to profusely apologize to Jesse Cates.

But it wasn't Jesse who hopped down from the seat of the high truck.

It was Sunny.

She wasn't smiling her usual bright smile. For the first time, she looked pissed off. Like really pissed off. Her brown eyes flashed with anger as she stomped toward him in an ordinary pair of scuffed brown cowboy boots that actually looked like they had been worn for more than just two-stepping at the Hellhole. Her cut-off shorts and T-shirt were splattered with paint and her hair was twisted up in some kind of messy bun that sprouted in all directions.

She looked hot.

Or maybe he was the one who was hot. He suddenly felt like he'd swallowed a shovelful of hot coals and they were burning their way through his body. The feeling only intensified when she poked him hard in the chest with her finger.

"What is it with you Mitchells running people off the road? And don't you dare try to make this out as my fault. I was minding my own business when you veered over on my side—" She thumped her chest and his gaze lowered to the swells of her full breasts in the pink lacy bra that was visible through the thin white cotton of her shirt. "My side! And believe me when I tell you that I'm over taking the blame for Mitchells who can't drive!"

He pulled his gaze away from her breasts and back to her flashing eyes. He had no problem dealing with fake-smiling, frivolous Sunny, but there was something about this fiery, angry Sunny that made him speechless.

"Well?" She crossed her arms, causing tempting cleavage to fill the vee neckline of her shirt. Out of nowhere a vision popped into his head of brushing his tongue between those two sweet swells before sucking the soft flesh into his mou—

He mentally shook himself.

What the hell, Reid. Get a grip!

He took a step back and cleared his throat. "You're right. I'm sorry. Are you okay? My insurance will pay for any damage to Jesse's truck." Although he figured that was unlikely given the huge push bumper on the front of the truck. The only things damaged were the flattened weeds.

She blinked those big brown eyes. "Did big bad Reid just apologize?"

He scowled. "Are you okay or not?"

"I'm fine." She glanced down at the cellphone in his hand. "But I now know where Sophie got her texting while driving. Cute pink rhinestone phone case, by the way."

He felt his cheeks flush. "It's not mine. It's

Sophie's. I got distracted reading her texts." And then even more distracted by a redheaded Daisy Duke. What was the matter with him? He had no business letting his libido sidetrack him from the problem at hand.

"You were reading her texts?" Sunny stared at him with horror. "You can't do that. That's like reading a girl's diary."

He glanced down at the phone. "Well, if it's any consolation I didn't understand a word of it. Do you know what johnnies are? Are they drugs?"

"Umm . . . no. They're not drugs."

Reid heaved a sigh of relief. "So what are they?"

Sunny hesitated. "Condoms."

His relief evaporated. "What!"

"I could be wrong. I'm not up on teenage texting lingo." She held out her hand. "Let me see what context they were used in."

"I thought you were appalled at me for reading Sophie's texts."

"Well, that was before I knew what she was texting. She's too young to be texting about condoms. Now let me see."

He handed the phone to her. "Maybe it's a joke. Maybe it's just her and her friend JC joking around."

Sunny read through the texts. "Nope. This doesn't sound like just joking around to me. It sounds like she has plans to meet this person tonight at Cooper Springs."

"Well, she can't. She's on restriction."

Sunny glanced up from the phone and shook her head. "Wow. You really are clueless, aren't you? I got in the most trouble on the nights I was on restriction."

"What do you mean?"

"I mean Sophie is obviously going to sneak out and meet JC."

"Like hell she will!"

"And how are you going to stop her? Are you going to lock her in her room? Stay up all night every night? Because I can tell you from experience that the more you try to stop a strong-willed teenager from doing something, the more they're going to try and do it."

He pushed back his hat and released an aggravated huff. "Then what am I supposed to do? Just let her have sex with some random guy when she's still struggling with losing her mama . . . and being stuck with an inept uncle who doesn't know shit about raising a teenager?"

"You don't have to do it alone, you know? Mimi and the Holiday sisters wanted to help."

"Thanks, but I'd just as soon not have my bosses in the middle of my family issues."

Sunny studied him for a long moment before she spoke. "What about me? Would you take help from me?"

He drew back. "What kind of help?"

She smiled slyly. "The kind of help that only a woman who understands wild teenagers can give you."

Chapter Eight

∽

"THIS IS RIDICULOUS."

Sunny glanced over her shoulder at Reid who was crouched behind her in the dark. She hadn't planned on volunteering to help him figure out what was going on with Sophie. Especially when she didn't like the man and he had made it perfectly clear he didn't like her. But the look of desperation in his eyes when talking about Sophie touched something in her heart. While he might not like her and she might not like him, it was obvious he cared for Sophie and was struggling to be a good guardian.

What kind of a person would she be if she ignored his plea for help?

Not to mention that it gave her something else to think about beside an empty gallery that needed to be filled with artwork.

"Lower your voice," she said in a hushed whisper. "Do you want Sophie to hear us?" She turned back to the trailer and the window they'd been waiting to open for the last twenty minutes.

She felt Reid shift behind her. His scent wafted over her as it had been doing ever since they'd crouched down in their hiding spot. It had taken her a while to figure out all the components. Definitely, horse and leather, but there were also hints of Irish Spring soap, Downy fabric softener, and some kind of musky cologne. The night of the party, there had been no cologne. She was positive. And she would have thought that if he wore cologne, he would wear it to a party. So why not then and why tonight when all he was going to be doing was spying on his niece?

Before she could come up with an answer, his warm breath fell against her ear and her panties melted. She'd always had this weird thing with her ears. It was like they were directly connected to her lady parts. Of course, not one man she had dated had figured that out. So there was no way Reid knew he was making her wet just by speaking low and sexy.

"This is a bad plan. I'm not going to hide in the dark like some silly teenager spying on my niece."

She tried to nonchalantly scoot away from him before her panties incinerated. "It's not spying. It's merely keeping a teen from doing something she really shouldn't be doing."

He shifted closer, his breath on her ear feeling at least ten degrees hotter and his manly scent twice as consuming. "Which I can do by simply confronting her about the texts I found on her phone."

"And like I told you numerous times, that will only tick her off even more and make her want to get back at you by having sex with JC. We need to get more information before we decide what to do."

"We?"

"Fine. You. And could you back off a little? You're crowding me."

"In case you didn't notice there's not a lot of room behind this rock. If I move farther away, Sophie will spot me when she climbs out the window. If she climbs out the window. I'm not so sure you know what you're talking about."

She turned to him, then wished she hadn't. He was close. So close the brim of his cowboy hat brushed the top of her head. She tried to scoot back, but the rock was behind her. So all she could do was stare into his gold-drenched eyes and try to act like she didn't feel like a stick of butter left out in the hot sun.

"Believe me, I know what I'm talking about. I've snuck out of more windows than I can count."

Those eyes narrowed. "What? Did you try to sneak out of every window in the big ol' mansion you grew up in?"

She wanted to laugh, but she wasn't about to let Reid know how she grew up. "I've always loved a good challenge . . . or maybe more of a good thrill."

There was a subtle shift that happened as soon as the words left her mouth. A shift she could sense more than see. A charged undercurrent filled the space between them. No man had ever made her tremble in her life and yet there was no other way to describe the quiver that ran through her as she looked into his eyes that had turned from a champagne gold to a molten gold.

"Are you cold?" he asked in a husky whisper.

Cold? She was about as far from cold as a person could get. She was burning up. Burning up with want for the man crouched in front of her. When his work-roughened hands closed around her bare arms and rubbed up and down, the trembling turned into more of a quaking.

It didn't matter that he didn't like her and she didn't much like him. She wanted him and she was tired of acting like she didn't. Angling her head beneath the brim of his hat, she moved toward those stern lips that had parted on a soft exhalation.

But before she could taste them, Reid's head jerked up and his eyes widened. "Shit! Sophie." He pushed her down behind the rock.

She'd had men on top of her before, but never with so much awareness. Her brain seemed to register it all at once. The sculpted planes of his chest pressed against her cheek, the cold hardness of his belt buckle pressed against her stomach, the tensing of his thighs on either side of her hips as he held most of his weight off her.

She had wanted him to touch her and, now that he was, she should be burning up with desire. But strangely enough, her desire had faded to a low throb while another emotion consumed her.

Calm.

Sunny had never been calm in her life. But that was the only way to describe the feeling that settled over her as she listened to the strong thump of Reid's heart beneath her ear. The closest she'd come to the feeling had been when she'd tried float therapy and spent time in an enclosed pod of warm water, just floating there and listening to her own heartbeat. But that had only calmed the antsy feelings inside her for a few minutes before she'd freaked out and buzzed for the attendant to let her out.

But there were no antsy feelings now. All she felt was a strong sense of security. Like nothing could ever harm her as long as she remained right where she was.

Which explained why she felt so disappointed when Reid pushed to his feet.

"Come on." He helped her up. "She's headed to Cooper Springs. As soon as I find out who this JC kid is, I'm going to give him a piece of my mind."

She was so dazed by her strange reaction to being in Reid's arms that it took a moment for his words to register. By the time they did, he was heading into the trees and she had to race to catch up with him.

She grabbed his arm and pulled him to a stop. "You can't just go charging in there and cause a scene."

"So I should just let her have sex with some yahoo?"

"No." She nibbled on her thumbnail. "We need to stop them without turning it into another thing you have to discipline her for."

"She should be disciplined for sneaking out."

She sighed. "Look, I know you think I'm just a

spoiled rich girl. But I've been in Sophie's shoes. I know what it's like to feel like your guardians don't care about you."

"I care about Sophie!"

Sunny shushed him. "I know you do, but she doesn't feel that. So you have to lighten up a little. In fact, it might be best if you let me handle this and you go on back to the trailer."

"Let you handle it? You're not her guardian."

"Exactly. So I can be more of her friend. And kids listen to friends more than they do parents."

He studied her with those penetrating eyes for a long moment before he nodded. "Okay."

She blinked. "Okay?"

"You have to be better at talking to her than I am. But I'm not going back to the trailer."

"Fine. But stay out of sight. I think I might have a plan."

He rolled his eyes. "Of course you do." He hesitated. "Did you hear that?"

She listened. "I don't hear anything."

He shook his head. "It was probably just the wind. So what's your plan?"

She smiled. "I'm just going to be ditzy me." She winked at him before she turned and headed through the trees. As she grew closer to Cooper Springs, doubts started to sneak in.

What was she doing? She didn't know anything about raising kids? Especially when she'd had such bad parental examples. But when she stepped through the trees and saw two figures standing by the edge of the springs, she knew she couldn't back out now. Sunny had had sex too soon and still regretted it. She had to at least try to help Sophie make a better decision.

She quietly moved closer so she could hear what they were saying.

". . . but I thought this was what you wanted," JC said.

"It is," Sophie replied. "But you didn't have to jump on me as soon as I showed up and start ripping my clothes off."

"I ripped your shirt?"

"Well, no, but you could have the way you were pawing me."

"Okay . . . well . . . then maybe we should take our shirts off."

"Yeah, maybe." But Sophie made no move to take off her shirt. And she jumped back when JC yanked his T-shirt over his head, making it quite obvious that she was having second thoughts about her decision.

Sunny knew exactly how she felt. All her life, she had jumped into things without thinking them through. More than once, she'd wished someone had been there to stop her. Not hesitating, Sunny strode out of the shadow of the trees, then stopped suddenly as if totally surprised.

"Oh!" She placed a hand on her chest. "Y'all scared me half to death. Sophie? Hey!" She walked over and pulled the young girl into her arms. She could feel her body shaking. Since it wasn't cold, Sunny figured it had more to do with nerves than temperature. She rubbed her back a few times before she drew away and smiled. "So I guess y'all had the same idea I had—a late-night swim." She cocked an eyebrow at JC who looked like he was about to pee his pants.

"Uhh . . . yeah . . . we were just going for a swim."

Sunny held out a hand. "Hey, I'm Sunny Whitlock. And you are?"

The kid moved his shirt to his other hand and gave Sunny's hand a brief shake. "Jared Carmichael."

"Nice to meet you, Jared. I hope you don't mind me crashing your swimming party."

"Uhh . . . no . . . actually, I was just getting ready to go." He pulled on his shirt. "I have baseball practice early tomorrow morning." He lifted a hand at Sophie. "See you later, Sophie."

Sophie didn't say a word until Jared was gone. Then she melted down on the ground and covered her face with her hands. "Nothing goes the way I plan. Nothing!"

Sunny sat down on a nearby rock. "I know what you mean. None of my plans worked out the way I'd hoped either."

Sophie lowered her hands and looked at her with stunned disbelief. "What are you talking about? Everything goes your way. You have tons of money and a big family who adores you and throws you the best birthday party ever and gave you your own cute apartment and your very own gallery. You have everything!"

"It does look that way, doesn't it? But just because something looks perfect that doesn't mean it is."

Sophie rolled her eyes. "So what's so unperfect

about your life? Did you break a nail this morning? Ran out of the flavored coffee you like?"

"I don't like coffee." She held out her hands. "And as you can see, I chew my nails to the quick—a nervous habit I can't seem to break."

"What do you have to be nervous about?"

She hesitated before she spoke the truth. "My family finding out I'm nothing but a fraud and all the paintings I said I sold are actually in a storage unit in Houston growing dust."

That seemed to get the smug look off Sophie's face. "You lied to your family?"

"Don't act so shocked. I believe you've been lying to your uncle about everything."

"That's different. I'm a teenager. You're an adult."

"Adults lie too. They're just better at hiding it."

Sophie scowled. "If you were so good at lying, my uncle never would have found out about me running you off the road."

"That was my bad—not because I told people, but for lying in the first place. That was wrong. We should have told your uncle the truth about what happened. You driving while texting could get people killed—you included. You needed to be held accountable for your actions."

"Well, I was. I can't have my cellphone for an entire month. Which I think is way too harsh."

"If you had run someone off the road and killed them, the penalty would be even harsher."

Sophie huffed. "You sound like my uncle."

"Well, he's right."

Sophie glared at her. "So now you're siding

with him? Just so you know, he thinks you're an entitled rich girl who doesn't know the value of money and is too stupid to come out of the rain."

Sunny couldn't help glancing back at the trees. "He said that?"

"Yeah, and a lot of other mean things too. So I wouldn't be siding with him if I was you. He hates everyone. He just likes horses and stupid cows." Sophie got to her feet and picked up a pebble, throwing it with all her might at the springs. It made a big splash before sinking to the bottom. "And he really hates kids."

"Maybe he doesn't hate kids. Maybe he just doesn't understand them." Sunny got to her feet and picked up a pebble. With a flick of her wrist, she tossed it at the springs and watched as it skipped across the glassy surface in moonlit ripples.

"Hey, how did you do that?"

"My brother Corbin taught me. It's all in the flip of the wrist." Sunny picked up another flat rock and held it out. "Hold it like this and try again."

Sophie took the rock and tried again. It skipped once before sinking. "It sounds like your brother is fun."

"Actually, Corbin was a lot like your uncle before he met his wife, Belle. He didn't have a lot of time for fun. He was too busy trying to make money to take care of me."

Sophie turned and stared at her. "Where were your parents?"

She skipped another stone. "My parents are two

people who really don't like kids ... or each other for that matter. When they got in fights and separated, they would pawn me and Corbin off on whatever relative would take us."

"That's shitty."

Sunny nodded. "Yep. It was pretty shitty. You think moving once and having to make friends at a new school is tough, try doing it eight times."

"Eight times?"

"It might have been seven. I lost count. But it doesn't matter. What matters is that your uncle didn't try to pawn you off, Sophie—even when he doesn't understand the first thing about taking care of a teenager. He kept you and he's trying his best to make you happy and give you a good life. So maybe you could help him out a little and try not to be so hard on him."

"Why do I have to be the one who is nice to him? Why can't he be nice to me? He's the adult. I'm just a kid who feels all ... icky inside. And I don't know why!" She burst out in tears.

Sunny pulled her into her arms and spoke in a soft voice. "Oh, honey, don't cry. You feel all icky inside because your mama died and you've been thrust into this new life with an uncle you don't really know. Not to mention, you have a bunch of teenage hormones racing around inside you, making you feel anxious and confused. But take it from someone who knows, doing bad things isn't going to make you feel better ... at least not in the long run. It might make you feel better at the time, but then it just makes you feel more icky."

Sophie drew back, her cheeks wet with tears. "What bad things did you do?"

Sunny hesitated, wondering just how much she should share with Sophie. She had already shared too much. But then she realized if she were going to help the teenager, she'd have to gain her trust. And the only way to do that was to be completely honest.

"I painted an extra *t* on the *But* on the Nothin' But Muffins sign and then almost peed my pants laughing when people drove by and did a double take."

Sophie's eyes widened before a giggle escaped. It was nice to see the solemn teenager smile. "You did that?"

She nodded. "I also stole a pair of the mayor's huge heart-covered boxer shorts off his clothesline and hoisted them up the flagpole at the town hall." When Sophie laughed harder, she continued. "And I stole Mrs. Stokes's Cadillac out of her driveway and parked it out in the middle of Mr. Milford's corn maze—I had a driver's license and wasn't texting while I did it, I might add."

"Oh my gosh, you were a hellion."

"Something I'm not proud of, Sophie. I did a lot of things I regret." She hesitated. "One of them was having sex before I was ready. Now I don't know what you were doing here tonight with that boy, but whatever it was, you didn't look like you were ready for it."

Sophie looked away and swiped at the tears on her cheeks. "I just wanted someone to like me."

"Yeah, well, like and lust are two different

things, honey. If you get them confused, you'll only end up getting hurt. Take my word for it."

Sophie looked back at her and nodded. "Please don't tell Uncle Reid. He doesn't even know I snuck out. In fact, I better get back before he discovers I'm gone."

Sunny should have let her go, but Sophie seemed so alone and lost, she couldn't do it. Sunny knew the feeling of not knowing where you belong in the world. Or if you belong in the world.

"Wait, Sophie." When she turned, Sunny shrugged. "Since you already snuck out, it seems a shame not to do something a little wild."

"Like what?"

Sunny smiled. "Have you ever gone skinny-dipping beneath a—" She looked at the sky. "Semi-full moon?"

Chapter Nine

REID HADN'T INTENDED to threaten a teenager. But when JC headed toward him, he couldn't help stepping out of the trees and issuing a warning.

"Stay away from Sophie, you little shit."

The kid startled and stumbled back, tripping over a rock and landing hard on his butt with a look of terror in his eyes. The terror grew when Reid's words were repeated in a loud, screeching voice.

"Little shit! Little shit!"

If the spreading wet spot on the front of the kid's jeans was any indication, he was scared pissless. Reid couldn't very well blame him. He was feeling a little scared himself as he glanced up into the dark trees where the voice had come from. As the teenager raced away like the hounds of hell were after him, Reid saw a movement on an oak limb.

"Who's there?"

"Bullshit!"

There was something about the tone of the voice that made Reid realize it wasn't human. He pulled his phone out of his pocket and turned on the flashlight, directing the light at the tree branches. Sure enough, a bird sat on the limb. A gray parrot that had no business being in an oak tree in the middle of a Texas ranch.

"What the fuck?"

The bird's beady eyes blinked. "Fuck! Fuck!"

Reid glanced around, wondering how the cussing parrot had gotten there. No one from either the Holiday Ranch or the Remington Ranch owned a parrot to his knowledge. It was too damn late to be calling around to see if they did. Which meant he would have to wait until the morning to figure it out. Until then, he'd just have to leave the bird where it was. Especially when he didn't have a clue how to get it down from the tree.

Turning, he headed back to the springs. He pulled up short when Sophie and Sunny weren't where he'd left them. Splashing had him glancing at the springs where he saw two bobbing heads in the water. One dark and one the color of a moonlit penny. He frowned. They shouldn't be having a swim party when Sophie needed a stern lecture about what she'd done.

But then Sophie laughed and all thoughts of lectures disappeared.

When was the last time he'd heard her laugh? Had he ever? Of course, why would she laugh around him when he'd done nothing but make her feel like she was an inconvenience—something he wanted out of his life? He'd given her nothing to laugh about. All he'd done was dish out orders and punishment . . . and resented her for keeping him from his dream.

But she wasn't responsible for her mother getting cancer. Or even for him becoming her guardian. He had made that choice. He had made it because his conscience wouldn't let him do otherwise. Which was a shitty reason for becoming a guardian.

Sophie was his only kin. The only one left in his family. He should be happy to have her in his life, instead of blaming her for inconveniencing him. She was just a kid. A kid whose entire life had changed overnight. Her mother had been sick and dying and, suddenly, this stranger showed up and started taking charge. No wonder he hadn't heard her laugh. He hadn't given her any reason to. He'd been an angry jerk who set down rules and didn't give an inch. A jerk who was all work and no play.

He needed to change that.

Unfortunately, he didn't have a clue how to go about making a teenager happy.

Another peal of laughter rang out and he glanced at the springs where Sophie and Sunny were frolicking.

But, obviously, Sunny did.

Maybe it was time to stop being such a stubborn fool and ask for help.

෴

The next morning, Reid got up early and made pancakes. He wasn't what anyone would call a great cook, but pancakes were something he could handle. Once he had the stack of pancakes plated, he decided to add a chocolate chip face to the top one like his mama had done for him as a kid.

It wasn't well received.

Sophie took one look at the grinning pancake and stared at him as if he'd grown horns.

"You don't like pancakes?" he asked.

"No. I like them . . . it's just a smiley face."

He shrugged. "You don't like smiles?"

She stared at him for a long moment before she shook her head and picked up her fork. She might not like the smiley face, but she seemed to like his pancakes. She finished the stack in record time and asked for seconds. He made a mental note to make pancakes more often—without the chocolate chip face.

On the way to school, he wanted to apologize for the way he'd been acting, but once again, he found himself tongue tied as he searched for the right words. It wasn't until he'd stopped in the pickup line and she started to get out that he finally spoke.

"Look, Soph, I get that I've been a real jerk. And I'm sorry. I'm gonna try to do better."

She stared at him again as if he was some kind of alien before she grabbed her backpack and jumped out. As he watched her merge into the crowd of teenagers, he thumped the steering wheel.

"Real smooth, Reid."

Before he headed back to the ranch, he stopped off at the sheriff's office. He figured if anyone knew what to do with a lost parrot, Melba would. As soon as he stepped in the door, she threw him a bright smile and held up one finger to indicate she would be with him after she finished the call she was on. He turned to sit down in one of the chairs in the waiting room and stopped short when he saw Sunny sitting there cuddling a little white-and-gray rabbit with one lop ear and deep brown eyes that matched Sunny's.

She looked as surprised to see him as he was to see her.

"Hey. What are you do—" She cut off and her eyes lit up. "You came for Patsy Cline!" She jumped up and pulled him into a hug that had him sucking in a deep breath of her sunshine scent. Before his brain could completely register how nice it felt to be in the arms of a beautiful woman—even with a wiggling rabbit between them—Sunny stepped back and gave him a devilish smile. "Thank the Lord you came to your senses. Now I don't have to implement my devious plan."

He blinked. "What devious plan?"

"I was going to leave Patsy in a basket on your stoop. I figured once you saw her, you wouldn't be able to resist her. I mean who could resist this sweet ball of fur." She lifted the squirming rabbit up to him.

He had to admit the bunny was cute. And the missing back foot did tug at his heartstrings. But he already had enough to deal with. He didn't need to add to it. "I didn't come here for Patsy Cline. I don't have time for a rabbit."

"Don't worry. Sophie has already promised to take full care of Patsy. We already worked it out."

His eyes narrowed. "You already worked it out?"

"Now don't be getting all grumpy. If Sophie has a sweet little bunny to keep her busy, she won't have time to sneak out." She cuddled the rabbit close, but Patsy wasn't having it. She started kicking her one back leg and wiggling to be put down. No doubt because Sunny was holding her wrong. As much as he shouldn't, Reid took the rabbit from her.

"Rabbits don't like to be held too tightly. You need to support their front paws and hips, but let their back feet dangle free so they don't have anything to instinctually push against." He demonstrated and Patsy stopped fighting and settled into the crook of his arm.

Sunny laughed as she smoothed the rabbit's ears. "I didn't realize you were a rabbit wrangler as well as a cow wrangler."

"The last ranch I worked at raised them."

She beamed. "Then it's a match made in heaven."

"Just what I was going to say." Melba came around her desk. "I'll just get Patsy's food, litter box, and crate."

Reid opened his mouth to stop her, but then quickly snapped it shut. Maybe Sunny and Melba were right. Maybe a pet was just what Sophie needed to help ease her grieving . . . and her dislike of him.

He didn't say a word as Melba scurried about

collecting Patsy's things. Until he remembered the real reason he'd come to the sheriff's office. "Have you heard anything about a lost parrot, Melba? There seems to be one living in a tree by Cooper Springs . . . yelling out profanity."

Sunny stopped petting Patsy and stared at him. "Wait a second. That was a parrot yelling *bullshit* the other night?"

"It appears so."

Melba laughed. "Sounds like a smart bird."

"Not smart enough to find its way home."

Melba set all of Patsy's things in a chair before she headed back to her desk. "I'll put the word out and see if I can't locate its owners. Until then, you might want to set out a bowl of water and some cut-up fruit and vegetables. We don't want the poor thing to starve to death."

Great.

Now Reid had a rabbit and a bird to care for.

A few minutes later, Patsy was in her crate and Sunny was helping him carry everything out to his truck. He made sure the crate was secure in the backseat before he closed the door and turned to her.

"I don't know if I should thank you or yell at you for sticking me with a pet I don't have time for."

"Now don't be a spoilsport. You're going to make Sophie one happy teenager."

He sighed. "I don't think one rabbit is going to fix all the damage I've done."

"Everything is fixable if you're willing to put in the time."

Reid wasn't so sure about that, but he appreciated Sunny's positivity. And that wasn't all he appreciated. "Thank you—not for the rabbit as much as what you did last night. You handled the situation much better than I would have."

Sunny's eyes widened. "Wait a second. Who are you? Gratitude and compliments? That's not the Reid Mitchell I've come to know."

He sent her an annoyed look. "You couldn't just accept my gratitude without making me feel like a jerk?"

"Nope."

He laughed. Her smile faded and she stared at him like he was a grinning chocolate chip pancake. "What?"

"I just haven't ever seen you laugh before." She reached out and pressed a finger to his lips. "I didn't think these had it in them."

All humor vanished as every cell in his body focused on the warm finger pressed to his mouth. He had tried damn hard not to think about how she had felt beneath him the other night—how all her soft curves had filled all his hard voids. But her touch had those repressed thoughts flooding his brain like a tidal wave. All he wanted to do was press her back against his truck and feel that perfect fit again.

She seemed to be of the same mind. It was easy to read the hot desire swirling in the depths of her pretty brown eyes. After a long, heated staring contest, her gaze lowered to his mouth and her tongue swept out and wet her lips.

It was a sultry invitation. One he really wanted

to take her up on. His mouth watered at just the thought of tasting those lips that were once again painted a soft pink. Would they taste like strawberry or bubble gum? He wanted more than anything to find out. But he had enough common sense left in his fantasy-filled brain to realize that would be a bad idea.

An extremely bad idea.

Unfortunately, before he could make his excuses and get the hell out of there, Sunny took matters into her own hands. With a needy moan that Reid felt all the way down to the toes of his boots, she replaced her warm finger with her soft, warm lips.

It was like pulling the trigger on a cocked gun.

The need and desire he'd been holding back exploded. Before he knew it, he had her shoved back against the truck, his hard body pinning her as his lips took what he wanted.

He wanted a lot.

He ravished her sweet mouth with hungry pulls of his lips and deep strokes of his tongue. She didn't taste like strawberries or bubble gum. She tasted like . . . sunshine, and he basked in her glow and heat like a man who had been living his entire life beneath a dark cloud. He never wanted to go back under that cloud. He wanted to stay right here, surrounded by this vibrant woman's energy forever.

He might have done just that if they hadn't been interrupted by a loud throat-clearing.

He drew away from Sunny to see Mrs. Stokes standing on the sidewalk in the ratty-looking fur she always wore. He blinked back to reality and realized what he'd been caught doing—mauling his boss's little sister smack dab in the middle of town.

He untangled his fingers from Sunny's hair and stepped away. He didn't know what to say so he just stood there feeling like a fool. Thankfully, Sunny came to his rescue. She pinned on a bright smile as if he hadn't almost taken her against his truck.

"Hey, Ms. Stokes! How are you doin' this fine day?"

Mrs. Stokes cocked a dark red eyebrow that matched her bouffant hair perfectly. "Not as good as you seem to be doing. A new gallery and now a new beau. Lucky girl."

Reid finally snapped out of his speechlessness "No! I'm not Sunny's beau. That was just . . ." He scrambled for an explanation for what had just happened, but came up empty.

Once again, Sunny jumped in. "All me." She shrugged. "What can I say? I have a hard time controlling my impulses."

Mrs. Stokes chuckled. "I understand completely. I never could control my impulses with hot cowboys either."

Sunny laughed before she sent the woman a pleading look. "I hope you'll keep this between us, Ms. Stokes. I would hate for word to get back to Corbin. He'll never let me hear the end of it if he finds out I accosted his foreman in the middle of town."

"It looked to me like Reid didn't mind much."

Mrs. Stokes shot him a calculating look before she returned her gaze to Sunny. "But you don't have to worry about me saying anything to Corbin. I have firsthand knowledge of how well your brother likes to control everyone in his life. Which reminds me. Please inform him that time is ticking on his part of our bargain. I understand he's been distracted by his new wife and their growing family, but a deal's a deal." She adjusted her fur around her shoulders. "Now if you'll excuse me, I have a hair appointment."

Once she was gone, Sunny turned to Reid. She looked thoroughly kissed. There were whisker burns around her mouth and her lipstick was completely gone and her lips slightly puffy. Even though she had been the one to make the first move, he owed her an apology for how quickly he'd let things get out of control.

"Look, Sunny, I'm sor—"

She pressed a finger to his lips once again. Once again, he had to fight the liquid desire that spread through him like a fast-acting drug.

"Let's not ruin a pleasant little interlude with a bunch of excuses for why it shouldn't have happened and why it can't happen again. I get it. You have a lot to deal with right now and you don't need any more complications. Believe me, I don't need any more complications in my life either." She removed her finger from his mouth and tapped his nose. "Now you better get your bunny home. I wish I could be there to see Sophie's face when she gets home from school and sees Patsy." She playfully socked him in the arm. "Good job,

Uncle Reid." She turned and headed to the big ol' monster truck that was parked a few spaces away.

He should be overjoyed that she hadn't made a big deal about the kiss.

But all he felt was a sad disappointment that he'd never taste sunshine again.

Chapter Ten

SOPHIE WAS RIGHT. Sunny was one lucky girl who should be thrilled with her blessed life. But it was hard to be thrilled when she knew she didn't deserve any of her blessings. Not when she had lied to everyone. And was continuing to lie to everyone.

She knew she needed to come clean, but how could she do that when Corbin had spent so much money on her becoming an artist? He'd paid for art classes, supplies, the art school and apartment in Paris, and now a gallery. She couldn't face the disappointment in his eyes when he realized he'd thrown all his money away on a failure. Especially when all she'd ever wanted to do was make him proud. And not just him, but Jesse and all the Holidays who had welcomed her into their family with open arms. What would they think of her if they found out she was nothing but a fraud and liar?

Punching her pillow in frustration, she sat up in bed and looked across the room at the painting sitting on the easel. She'd painted it last night when she got back from packing up her apartment in Houston. It had started out as a painting of Jesse and Liberty's pug, Buck Owens, frolicking in the fields behind the carriage house. It had ended up another "angry art" painting—a graffiti mishmash of mars black and yellow ochre and copper gold and Bordeaux red. Although, in the morning light, the splatters and slashes resembled two people kissing.

She wasn't surprised.

The last few days, when she wasn't thinking about being a failure, she was thinking about kissing. Or not kissing as much as one kiss. One hot, steamy, knock-your-knickers-off kiss.

She had kissed a lot of men in her life, but not one had ever kissed her like Reid. Not one had kissed her as if his life had depended on it—as if he'd been walking through a hot, barren desert for days and she was a tall glass of water he needed to drain dry or he'd die. Of course, once Mrs. Stokes interrupted them, Reid had acted like the kiss had been the worst mistake of his life.

And it was a mistake.

Reid wasn't just some guy she could have a fling with and go on her merry way. He was Corbin's assistant ranch manager. Sophie's guardian. Getting involved with him was wrong on so many levels. Especially when Sunny had never been good at relationships. She was too flighty. After only a few dates, she was always ready to move on. If Reid was as flighty as she was that would be one thing. But it didn't take a degree in psychology to know he was the type of man who took commitments seriously.

He was stable and reliable and honest.

Everything Sunny wasn't.

A rap on the door startled her out of her thoughts and she quickly jumped out of bed to cover her angry art. She had just finished throwing a drop cloth over it when Liberty appeared at the top of the stairs.

"Good mornin'!" Liberty glanced at the covered painting Sunny hovered around. "Is that something new?"

"Uhh . . . yes, but I'm not finished with it yet."

"Well, I'd love to see it when you are. We need a piece of art to hang in the entryway. That looks like the perfect size." Liberty glanced at the empty boxes in the corner. "So did you get all moved in?"

"I didn't have a lot to move. I travel pretty light. Something you learn when you move as much as I do."

Jesse had obviously told his wife about Sunny and Corbin's vagabond childhood because Liberty's green eyes turned sad. "Well, you can start collecting things now. Jesse made sure you have plenty of storage. And speaking of things in storage, I came to get the trunk Jesse left in your closet."

Sunny had seen the trunk as she was unpacking and putting away her clothes. Of course, her curiosity had gotten the best of her and she'd opened it.

"Why does Jesse want to keep a bunch of old letters?" she asked.

"They belong to Mrs. Fields. Jesse discovered them when he was cleaning out the attic before renovations and thinks our guests would love reading through them. But what your brother thinks is appropriate for guests and what really is appropriate might be two different things. So I want to read them first."

Sunny laughed. "You have a good point. You want help?" Anything to get her mind off her inability to paint . . . and an incinerating kiss that could never be repeated.

An hour later, Sunny and Liberty were sitting on the bed sharing salacious excerpts from the letters spread around them.

"Dearest Fanny," Sunny read. "I can't forget the night we spent together. Your lips were like two sundrenched rose petals that brought me to rapturous fulfillment. I look forward to feeling those lips . . . and that fulfillment again next Saturday night. Yours truly, Nathanial Davenport."

"Nathanial Davenport?" Liberty took the letter from Sunny and examined it. "I wonder if he was the same Nathanial Davenport who started the First Baptist Church."

Sunny laughed. "If it is, it sounds like he had plenty to repent about on Sunday morning."

"Since Nathanial's descendants probably don't want to read about their great-great-great grandfather receiving a blow job from the town's notorious madam, this one should probably go in the reject pile." Liberty leaned over the bed and placed the letter in the trunk with the other rejected letters. "Along with the one about how much fun the mayor of the town had with two of Mrs. Fields's 'finest ladies.'"

"It certainly sounds like people had lots of fun in these rooms." Sunny pulled a paper clip off two letters. She set one on the bed next to her and opened the other one. Her eyes widened as she read the typed words. "Although this one doesn't sound fun as much as intriguing. 'Dear Mrs. Fields. Here is your payment as per our arrangement. I expect you to handle the situation with the utmost confidentiality and discretion. If word gets out to anyone, I'll consider our agreement broken and won't hesitate to make sure your establishment closes for good.'"

Liberty's eyes widened. "Wow, that sounds more threatening than intriguing. Who signed it?"

She looked at the bottom. "Just initials. U.T."

"University of Texas?" Liberty laughed.

"Maybe the letter that was paper-clipped to it will give us more information." Sunny placed the letter back in the envelope and set it on the nightstand before she picked up the paper-clipped letter. But before she could open it, Noelle came up the stairs carrying a bakery box.

"Hey! What are y'all doin'?"

"We're just going through some old letters we found in the attic," Liberty said. "I hope those are muffins. I sent Jesse for some hours ago, but he obviously got sidetracked. I swear the man stops and talks with everyone."

Noelle held up the box she carried. "Your muffins have arrived. And Jesse did get sidetracked talking to the townsfolk, but it was hard not to when everyone was standing in the street looking at the café sign."

"Did you get a new sign?"

Noelle sighed. "No, but, once again, some prankster teens thought it would be funny to add a *t* to the *But*."

The letter slipped from Sunny's hand as she stared at Noelle. "What?"

"You don't remember?" Noelle said. "I think we were freshmen in high school and someone painted a *t* on the sign turning it into Nothin' Butt Muffins."

Sunny tried to keep her face completely devoid of emotions. "Do you know who did it?"

Noelle shook her head. "Just like last time, the culprit got away with it. But I'm sure it's teenagers again. Although whoever did it before was a much better painter. This time, the *t* looks more like an *j* and they splattered paint everywhere."

"Too bad," Liberty said. "If it looked like a *t*, I'd convince you to keep it. It's damn funny."

Noelle scowled. "It's not funny when you had to spend all morning filling out a police report with Decker when you should be baking. And are you comparing my baking to a butt, Libby?"

"Never." Liberty held out her hands. "Now give me."

Noelle held the box back. "Sunny first. I don't want you eating Sunny's Strawberry Sweet Cakes in a pregnancy hunger frenzy."

Sunny graciously took the muffin from the box Noelle held out to her, even though her stomach felt like a jar of nervous bees. "A police report?

Are you sure that's necessary? I'll be more than happy to repaint the sign for you. Like you said, it was probably just an innocent prank."

"Thank you, Sunny. That would be awesome. And maybe it was an innocent prank, but we can't just let it go. Last time, when Sheryl Ann let it go, whoever was responsible just kept right on causing problems. And I can't see our mayor being thrilled if her underwear ends up flying from the town hall flagpole. Especially when we all know she wears Spanx."

Unable to sit still a second longer, Sunny jumped to her feet, startling both Noelle and Liberty.

"I just remembered. I have a . . . nail appointment." She waggled the fingers of the hand not holding the muffin. "I think it's about time to cover these unsightly things with acrylic." With her brightest smile, she turned and headed for the closet to get dressed.

It didn't take her long to get to the high school. Just stepping into the halls brought back all the inferior feelings she'd had when she'd gone there. Once again, she felt like an outsider who would never really fit in—especially when she found herself standing in front of Miss Burrows.

The office receptionist hadn't changed at all. She was still as skinny as a pencil, still wore the same large black-framed glasses . . . and was still as mean as a rattlesnake.

"If you want to talk to the principal, you're out of luck." She continued to type away on her computer keyboard, not even glancing in Sunny's direction. "He's busy."

Sunny fidgeted. "Actually, I was hoping to talk with Sophie Mitchell."

Miss Burrows stopped typing and sent her the same look she'd sent her years before when Sunny had come into the office—like she was an airhead who didn't understand the simplest of rules. "I'm sorry, Miss Whitlock, but we don't just let random people take our students out of class to talk to them."

"I know that, Miss Burrows, but I just need to talk to her for a second. And I'm not random. You've known me since I was a freshman. Remember?"

A distasteful look crossed her wrinkled face. "Oh, I remember you. I constantly caught you in the halls when you should have been in class."

"I had passes."

Miss Burrow scowled. "Ones I'm sure you finagled from your teachers. You fooled a lot of people with your sweet smile, young lady. But you never fooled me. Now if you'll excuse me, I have work to—"

She cut off as Jace walked into the office wearing his coaching polo shirt and carrying a clipboard. Sunny hadn't known Jace in high school. He'd already left for college by the time she and Corbin had come to town and had only recently returned—much to the entire town's happiness. He had been, and still was, the hometown football hero. Only now he was coaching instead of playing. Hallie said he'd been one depressed grumpy Gus when his professional football career had ended. He wasn't depressed or grumpy now. Every time Sunny ran into him, he looked like a man who had everything he wanted in life.

A man who had no trouble fitting in.

A big smile spread over his face when he saw her. "Hey, Sunny. What are you doing here?"

"I just stopped by to talk to Sophie Mitchell." She glanced at Miss Burrows. "But I forgot that . . . random people can't take students out of class."

Jace nodded. "Yeah, that is frowned upon." He flashed a smile at Miss Burrows and Sunny was shocked to see the woman blush. "Thank you, Miss Burrows, for protecting our students. I know everyone at this school feels safer with you sitting behind that desk with your strict guidelines and lovely smile." Miss Burrows's blush got even brighter. "Sophie has English this period, right?"

"No, History. But I can't let—"

Jace held up a hand. "Of course you can't. I'll be happy to walk Sunny out." Except as soon as they were out of the office, he led her in the opposite direction of the front doors. He stopped a few feet away from a classroom and turned to her.

"Hallie told me about the sisters' plans to make Sophie feel more welcome here. She also told me that Reid made it perfectly clear he didn't need the help. And if Reid doesn't want help, Sunny, maybe we should leave things alone."

Sunny wished she could. But it was too late for that. She'd butted her nose in where it didn't belong and now Sophie was going to pay the price. She couldn't let that happen.

"I totally agree, Jace, but I just need to talk with Sophie for a second." She gave him the same pleading look she'd given all her teachers when she'd gotten antsy in class and wanted out.

A twinkle entered Jace's eyes. "Now I know why Corbin gives you everything you want. Okay, I'll get Sophie for you. But I still don't think it's a good idea. Reid doesn't seem like the type of man who will put up with people interfering in his life."

Sunny knew that better than most. If Reid found out she was behind Sophie's prank . . . well, she wasn't sure what he would do. But it wouldn't be good. Which was why she was there. Hopefully, she could correct her mistake before things got too out of hand.

Unfortunately, things had already gotten out of hand.

The click of boot heels had Sunny turning to see Principal Tucker and Sheriff Decker Carson stepping out of the office. She said a silent prayer that they would head in the opposite direction.

They didn't. They headed straight toward Jace and Sunny. And she knew in her heart of hearts the sheriff wasn't there to give a talk on bicycle safety. She watched in horror as he and the principal stopped at the door she and Jace stood next to. Decker nodded a grim greeting to them both before he followed the principal inside the classroom.

A classroom that held Sophie Mitchell.

Chapter Eleven

WHEN REID GOT the call from Sheriff Carson, his first thought had been that someone had witnessed him running Sunny off the road. The thought that Sophie had snuck out of the trailer and vandalized a business in town had never even crossed his mind.

But he was looking at the proof on the sheriff's laptop screen that very second. The camera on the bank ATM across the street had caught the entire thing. Reid watched as the shadowy figure snuck across the roof of Nothin' But Muffins with a can of paint and a paintbrush. When Decker zoomed in, there was Sophie wearing Reid's black winter stocking cap and a big ol' smile.

He turned to Sophie who sat slumped in the chair next to his. "What—?" He cut off when he realized he'd started the question wrong. It was obvious *what* she'd been doing. "Why? Why would you climb up on the roof of the town bakery and deface a sign? It makes absolutely no sense whatsoever."

Sophie picked at a hole in the knee of her jeans. He couldn't help feeling responsible for her wearing holey jeans as much as he felt responsible for her defacing a sign. "I was trying to make the icky feeling go away," she muttered.

"The icky feeling? What icky feeling?"

She sighed. "Never mind. You wouldn't understand."

He tried to hold in his anger, but damned if he could. "You're right. I don't understand. I don't understand at all." He pointed at the screen of the laptop. "I don't understand why someone would want to do that—icky feeling or no icky feeling. It's childish and irresponsible and just plain . . . stupid!" He wanted the word back as soon as it left his mouth, but it was too late.

Sophie lifted her gaze and he could read the hurt in her hazel eyes. "Stupid? Well, you're stupid too. You're a stupid, stupid stupid!" She burst into tears.

Reid rubbed a hand over his jaw and released a frustrated sigh as Decker closed his laptop and pulled a tissue from a box on his desk.

"Okay. How about if everyone takes a deep breath for a second?" He handed the tissue to Reid. Talk about stupid. It took him a good full minute and a questioning look from Decker before he figured out the sheriff wanted him to hand it to Sophie. Of course, when he tried to, she slapped it away.

"I don't want anything from you!"

Reid crumpled the tissue in his fist with frustration just as Melba tapped on the door and stuck her head in.

"Sorry to interrupt, Sheriff, but Sunny Whitlock is here and she says she really needs to talk to you."

"Tell her I'll be out when I'm through here," Decker said.

Melba hesitated. "Umm . . . she wants to talk to all three of you."

"No!" Reid spoke a little too loudly, but all he needed was Sunny Whitlock adding to this drama. Although the information that Sunny was there had caused Sophie to stop crying. So maybe she could help. Reid certainly didn't know how to handle this.

Decker got up from his chair. "I'll just go see what she needs." He shot Reid a sympathetic look. "That will give you and Sophie some time to talk privately."

Once he was gone, Reid turned to Sophie. Her tears had caused her makeup to smear and run. He held out the crumpled tissue. "You have . . . umm . . ." He waved a finger around his eye.

She jerked the tissue from his hand and proceeded to wipe her eyes and make an even bigger mess. Obviously, she wasn't very good at cleaning up messes. Of course, neither was he. It seemed to be a family trait.

"Look, I wasn't calling you stupid, Soph. I was saying what you did was stupid. And you have to agree that it was pretty stupid. You can't go around vandalizing people's property just because you have some bad feelings. If you have a bad feeling, you just need to deal with it. Bad feelings are part of life."

She stared at him as if he'd just given her the

worst advice ever. "That's it? That's what life is? Just feeling bad and dealing with it?"

When repeated back to him, he had to admit it sounded depressing as hell. "Well, no. There are good things about life too."

"Really? Like what? Because, so far, my life hasn't had too many of those."

His hadn't either, but he figured now wasn't the time to point that out. "Climbing on a rooftop and vandalizing a sign is only going to make things worse not better." A thought struck him. "How did you get up there anyway?"

"I climbed up on the dumpster just like—" She cut off.

"Just like what? Was someone with you? Was it that JC kid who talked you into doing this?"

Before she could answer, the door opened and Decker walked back in . . . with Sunny. Reid blamed the dip his stomach took on embarrassment that, once again, he couldn't handle his teenage niece. It had nothing to do with those mile-long legs showing beneath the hem of her sundress. Or the sexy way her hair fell around her smooth bare shoulders. Or the way she nibbled on her plump bottom lip.

She looked . . . nervous. He instantly became wary.

"Go ahead, Sunny," Decker prompted. "Tell them what you told me."

Sunny cleared her throat. "So Sophie isn't really responsible for what happened . . . I mean she is responsible, but she . . . might have had some help planning it."

Reid looked back at Sophie. "So it was that JC kid who came up with this."

"No," Sunny said. "I did . . . it was my idea."

He thought he was confused before. It was nothing compared to now. "Your idea?"

She smiled weakly. "Pretty much."

Reid was so angry he was surprised steam wasn't pouring out of his ears. He had trusted Sunny to help him with Sophie and instead she had convinced Sophie to pull some airheaded prank.

He jumped up. "What the hell?"

Decker quickly stepped between him and Sunny. "I think we all need to remain calm and talk this out like adults."

That was almost laughable.

"Adults?" Reid said. "How can we possibly talk this out like adults when we obviously aren't all adults?" He was talking about both Sophie and Sunny, but Decker didn't take it that way.

"Good point. Sophie, why don't you go out and wait in the lobby. Melba has a new kitten I'm sure she'll let you play with."

Sophie didn't wait to be asked twice. She scurried out like her tail was on fire. Once she was gone, Decker waved at the chairs in front of his desk. "Please sit down, you two. I'm sure we can get this figured out."

Sunny took a chair, but Reid was too angry to sit. It was all he could do to keep from cussing a blue streak and punching a wall. "I trusted you to talk some sense into Sophie and instead you talked her into doing something even worse."

Sunny's eyes widened. "Now I wouldn't say painting a sign is worse than having sex before you're ready. And I didn't talk her into it. I merely told her about how I had dealt with my icky feelings."

"Icky feelings! What are these icky feelings y'all keep talking about?"

"They are feelings that make you feel icky."

"I gathered that much, but what does icky mean?"

"That's the problem. It's hard to explain to someone who has never had to deal with feeling icky. They are just these overwhelming feelings that consume you and you feel like you'll go crazy if you don't do something to get rid of them. When I was in high school, doing pranks was what made me feel better. But when I told Sophie about them, I didn't think she'd try them out."

"So you were the one who painted the sign before?" Decker asked.

Sophie's face flushed a guilty pink. "Yes."

"And hoisted the mayor's boxers up the flagpole and painted a tutu and princess crown on the mural of the snarling wildcat on the side of the gym."

When she nodded, Decker sat back in his chair and covered his mouth with his hand. His twinkling eyes were a dead giveaway that he was trying hard not to laugh his ass off.

Reid didn't find it amusing. He was struggling to raise his niece and had trusted this woman to help him. Instead, she had sabotaged him. And it didn't help that every time he looked at her all he could think about were the taste of her lips, the silkiness of her hair, and the press of her hot—

There was a tap on the door and, once again, Melba stuck her head in. "Sorry, to keep interrupting, Sheriff, but your wife and daughter stopped by to see you."

Decker's face lit up as he sprung out of his chair. "If you'll excuse me, I'll be right back."

As soon as the door clicked closed behind him, Reid turned to Sunny to give her hell. But when he saw her face, his angry words fizzled. For once, she didn't look like her namesake. She looked like a rain cloud that was about to burst.

"I'm sorry," she said in a low whisper. "I thought I was helping by letting Sophie know she wasn't alone—that I have icky feelings too. I honestly didn't think she would pull the same stupid prank I pulled." She slumped in the chair and stared down at her clutched hands in her lap.

He had never really looked at her hands. Probably because there were so many other parts of her body that held his attention. So he was more than a little surprised to see her fingernails chewed down to the quick. The realization that she had a nervous habit stunned him. She always seemed so self-assured. But it appeared that she hid her nerves as well as she hid her . . . icky feelings. The realization caused his anger to fizzle out.

He sat down in the chair and sighed. "It's not your fault. It's mine. If I was a better guardian, this wouldn't have happened." He rubbed a hand over his face. "I thought things were better between us. This morning, she gave me a smile—an actual smile—when I teased her about spoiling Patsy rotten. But, obviously, I still suck at making her happy."

"It's not all about you, Reid. Sophie is dealing with a lot right now. Her mother dying, moving to a new town, making new friends, and teenage hormones. You're not completely responsible for her happiness. She needs to figure out how to deal with her own emotions and problems."

He lowered his hand and looked at her. "By vandalizing signs?"

Sunny blushed. "I tried to tell her that didn't work for me, but I guess she wanted to try it out for herself."

He glanced down at her nails. "What did work for you?"

She folded her fingers, hiding her nails from his gaze. He didn't know why that bothered him so much. But it did. "Art. I found art. Painting calms me . . . and extreme sports."

"Extreme sports?"

"Skydiving, bungee jumping, rock climbing."

"You've done all those things?"

She nodded. "I'm a bit of a thrill seeker."

It was pathetic how just the word *thrill* coming from her lips had his mind going down a road it had no business going down. Kissing her had been thrilling. More thrilling than anything he'd ever done in his life. He couldn't help but want to experience that thrill again.

His gaze lowered to her mouth. A mouth that had haunted his dreams ever since he'd tasted its welcoming warmth. She wore no glossy pink lipstick today, but her natural rose-colored lips were just as tempting. Her tongue swept out to wet them and he lifted his gaze to find her watching him with an intensity that had his heart knocking against his rib cage as if fighting to get out.

He knew it was mistake, but he couldn't seem to stop himself from leaning closer to their beckoning softness. She leaned forward too. Their lips were only a breath apart when the door opened.

They quickly turned away from each other as Decker stepped into the room. Completely unaware of the sexual energy swirling around, he sat down in his chair and folded his hands on the desk.

"Alright. So seeing as how this is Sophie's first offense, I don't think there's any reason to involve the juvenile system. Unless you disagree, Reid."

Reid shifted in his chair and tried to keep his gaze off the woman sitting next to him. "No. I'd appreciate if you didn't involve them."

"That still doesn't mean Sophie gets off scot free. She'll have to do some community service."

"I think that's only fair."

Decker nodded. "I'm glad we're on the same page." He glanced at Sunny who looked as flushed as Reid felt. "I think you should do community service as well."

Sunny blinked. "Me?"

"You did pull the same prank." He cocked an eyebrow. "And a lot more. I think the townsfolk will forgive you much faster if you show you're sorry for what you did by doing community service."

"But nobody knows about me doing those pranks except you, me, Reid, and Sophie."

Decker sighed. "And Melba. She has a tendency to listen at the door. And while she's a kindhearted, good woman, she isn't exactly what you'd call tight lipped."

If Reid had thought Sunny looked like a sad rain cloud before, it was nothing compared to what she looked like now. She looked like her entire world had come crashing down around her. He couldn't help sympathizing. Folks would forgive a teenager for a one-time offense much more easily than an adult who had pulled the wool over their eyes for years.

"Maybe you could talk to Melba," he said. "And ask her not to say anything."

Decker looked at him. "And what kind of example would that be for Sophie?"

"He's right," Sunny said. "I should pay for what I did too. It's only fair."

Decker got to his feet. "Then if that's settled, I'd like to talk to Sophie alone and make sure she understands that if she causes any more trouble, I won't be as lenient."

Reid stood and held out his hand. "Thank you, Sheriff Carson. I appreciate you giving Sophie a second chance."

Decker shook his hand. "Everyone deserves a second chance. And call me Decker."

When Reid stepped out into the lobby with Sunny, he found Sophie sitting on the floor with a kitten curled on her lap. Since getting Patsy Cline, Reid had learned that his niece was an animal person. She and Patsy had taken to each other like ducks to water. Sophie was rarely without the rabbit tucked in her arm. Even now, she seemed reluctant to let go of the cat. She held it close to her chest as she got to her feet, her attention focused solely on Sunny.

"You didn't have to tell the truth. I wouldn't have tattled."

Sunny reached out to pet the kitten. "I know, but I couldn't have lived with myself if I let you take all the blame. I shouldn't have told you about the pranks."

"You just wanted me to feel better. You didn't make me do it. It was my decision." Sophie hesitated and finally looked at Reid. "What's gonna happen to me?"

Before Reid could answer, Decker spoke. "I'll be happy to answer that. Come on in to my office, Sophie."

Sophie nodded solemnly and placed the kitten back in its crate. She started for Decker's office and then stopped and threw her arms around Reid.

"Please don't let them take me to jail, Uncle Reid! Please! I promise I'll never do anything bad again."

It was the first time she'd ever hugged him and he didn't know what to do. He awkwardly patted her back as his heart tightened with an emotion he couldn't describe. "It's okay. You're not going to jail, Soph."

She drew back, her eyes tear drenched and heartbreaking. "And you're not gonna get rid of me? You're not gonna put me in foster care?"

Emotion welled up inside him and it was a struggle to keep the tears from his own eyes. "Hell, no. Where would you get that crazy idea? We're family, Soph. Family sticks together through thick and thin." He tucked a strand of hair behind her ear. "We're in this together, kid. You're not going anywhere ... and neither am I."

Chapter Twelve

On Saturday morning, Sunny woke to rhythmic knocking on her attic room door. It was a knock she'd recognize anywhere. Ever since she had met Jesse, he rapped out "You Are My Sunshine" whenever he knocked on her doors. It always made her smile.

And this morning was no different . . . even though she had lots of reasons for not smiling. Mainly, the fact that everyone in town would soon find out she was the devious prankster who had destroyed signs and caused all kinds of trouble for them.

So far, Jesse was the only family member who knew. Since he had been a little bit of a rascal himself growing up, she figured he would understand her devious side. That, and she'd needed help taking down the Nothin' But Muffins sign the night before and bringing it here so she could start painting it.

Jesse hadn't been surprised to hear about her misdeeds. Apparently, he was like Miss Burrows and knew there was more behind Sunny's bright smile than met the eyes. Unlike Corbin, who thought Sunny hung the moon and never did anything wrong. He'd soon find out how wrong he'd been and she was not looking forward to his look of hurt and disappointment.

The knock came again and she lifted her head and groggily called, "Come in, Jess!" before snuggling back in her pillow. There was a click of boot heels on stairs. A lot of boot heels. She popped up like a Jack in the Box worried that Corbin had come with Jesse. But it wasn't her brother who followed Jesse up the stairs.

It was Reid and Sophie.

Sunny was relieved and also embarrassed about being caught looking like a sleep-wrinkled hot mess when Reid looked like every woman's fantasy in his black Stetson, muscle-popping white T-shirt, and form-fitting Wranglers. She wasn't sure if she blushed from embarrassment or the way his champagne eyes slid over her.

But she had decided that Reid was one wicked desire she couldn't give in to. Not only because she worried about hurting him and Sophie, but also because she worried about getting hurt herself.

The desire she had for Reid was much stronger than anything she'd felt before. In Decker's office, she'd been seconds away from throwing herself at him just like she'd done in the middle of town. Her intense feelings scared her enough to want to stay away from him. Thankfully, he was only dropping Sophie off to help her paint the sign.

Sunny climbed out of bed. "Sorry. I overslept." She sent an annoyed look at Jesse for bringing them up without making sure she was awake and dressed, but he was too busy laughing to notice.

"Nice jammies, Sunshine Brook."

Too late, she realized what pajamas she'd thrown on last night. She felt her cheeks heat once again as Reid took in the *Elf* onsie Noelle had gotten her for Christmas. He pressed his lips together as if he was trying to keep his own laughter in as Sophie exclaimed,

"I love Buddy! Those are the cutest pajamas ever!"

Sunny ignored the men and smiled brightly at Sophie, who was cradling Patsy Cline in her arms. "Thank you, Soph. I love them too." She reached out and slid her hand over the rabbit's soft ears. "It will just take me a second to get dressed. You and Patsy make yourselves at home." She glanced at Reid. "I'll drop her off at the ranch when we're finished here." She expected him to nod and head for the door. Instead, he took off his hat.

"I think I'll stay if it's all the same to you."

It wasn't the same to Sunny. He was pure temptation and she had never been good at ignoring temptation. But she couldn't be rude. Especially when she understood perfectly why he wanted to stay. He didn't want her putting any more bad ideas into Sophie's head.

She shrugged. "Suit yourself. I'll just be a minute."

She wasted no time changing into her painting clothes and braiding her hair. She emerged from the bathroom only a few moments later to find

Sophie sitting on the bed looking bored as Reid talked to Jesse about spring branding.

Jesse had been a professional rodeo cowboy so it made sense that Reid would talk ranching with him. What didn't make sense was the way Sunny felt as she listened to Reid confidently lay out his plan for getting all the new calves vaccinated and tagged.

She loved helping out at the ranch, but people talking about it had never made her feel all breathless and lightheaded. The feeling only intensified when Reid glanced over and their eyes locked. He cut off in mid-sentence and there was this charged silence, similar to the one in Decker's office, before he pulled his gaze away and returned to his conversation with Jesse.

"I guess you think cowboying is as dumb as I do."

Sunny took a moment to regain her equilibrium before she turned to Sophie. "Actually, I kind of like it. What don't you like about it? Don't tell me you don't like riding horses."

The teenager shrugged as she stroked Patsy's head. "I've never ridden. Horses . . . scare me."

Sunny wasn't surprised. She'd been a little scared of them too at first. "They are big and intimidating." She nodded at the rabbit. "But they're animals just like Patsy. Show them love and respect and they'll show the same to you." She sat down on the bed. "I bet you were surprised when you came home from school to find Patsy."

A guilty look settled on Sophie's features. "I guess I didn't do such a good job of showing my appreciation."

"I have to agree. Painting the sign wasn't a good way to thank your uncle for getting you a cute pet." She hesitated. "But maybe you can come up with another way."

"Like what?"

"Like being helpful and nice rather than being belligerent and mean. Your uncle is doing the best he knows how."

Sophie's shoulders slumped. "I know. It was a stupid—" She cut off and cringed.

"What's wrong? Did Patsy kick you?"

"No. I . . ." Sophie glanced over at Reid and Jess before she looked back at Sunny and lowered her voice. "I have really bad cramps."

"Ahh," Sunny said. "Those are no fun, are they? Did you take some ibuprofen?"

Sophie shook her head. "We were out."

"Well, you need to take some." She got up. "Slip off your shoes and climb on up in bed and rest while I get you a couple."

"I can't rest. I don't want Uncle Reid thinking I'm trying to get out of painting the sign."

"You'll still get to help with the sign. I promise you'll feel much better when the painkillers kick in." Sunny plumped up the pillows against the headboard. "Now climb on in here. I'll deal with your Uncle Reid."

Sophie hesitated for only a second before she slipped off her sneakers. Once she was propped up on the pillows, Sunny went to straighten the covers around her when she noticed Mrs. Fields's letter on the nightstand. In all the excitement yesterday, she'd forgotten all about it. She picked it up and slipped it into her back pocket to give to Liberty later.

"What's going on?"

She turned to see Reid staring at Sophie propped up in the bed. "Sophie isn't feeling well and she's going to rest a little before she starts painting."

"But—"

She cut him off. "No buts, no cuts, no coconuts. And since you decided you want to be here, you can help me while she's resting. See those cans sitting on the counter? They need to be opened and stirred." She glanced at his white T-shirt. "And unless you want a paint-splattered shirt, you'll need to get on one of the paint shirts hanging on those hooks."

Reid's dark eyebrows lowered, but he didn't say a word before he turned to the hooks where the shirts hung.

Jesse cleared his throat. "Well, it looks like y'all got things under control here so I think I'll go. I never have been good at painting. I just throw it on and hope for the best." If Sunny's angry paintings were any indication, they had that in common. He turned to Reid who was picking out a shirt. "Make sure you call me when spring branding starts." His eyes twinkled when he glanced at Sunny. "And maybe we can get Sunny and Sophie to help as part of their community service. I'm already putting together a list of things they can do around here to present at the next town council meeting."

Sunny rolled her eyes. "Gee, thanks."

He reached out and tugged on her braid. "What are big brothers for if not to make their sister's life miserable?" He waved at Reid. "See ya, Reid." He winked at Sophie. "Feel better, squirt."

Once he was gone, Sunny got Sophie some painkillers and water. When she came out of the bathroom, Reid was standing on the other side of the room . . . shirtless.

She froze in her tracks.

She had expected him to put a paint shirt on over his T-shirt, but it looked like she hadn't made that clear. The naked muscles of his back flexed and released in a display of stunning masculinity as he slipped his arms in the sleeves of the shirt and pulled it over his broad shoulders.

It wasn't until she felt something cold splashing her bare toes that she realized she was spilling the glass of water she held. She closed her eyes and took a deep, even breath before she turned to the bed. Sophie was fast asleep with Patsy Cline cuddled against her neck. After leaving the painkillers and water on the nightstand, Sunny turned to see Reid standing there with a concerned look on his face.

"She never said a word about feeling sick. Do I need to take her to the doctor?"

"She doesn't need to go to the doctor. It's just menstrual cramps."

Reid's face flamed. "Oh."

His embarrassment made Sunny realize how

difficult it must be for a single man to suddenly be thrown into a teenage girl's world. Or vice versa. It had to be hard on Sophie too, living with a man who didn't understand her needs. But there wasn't anything Sunny could do about it. She had tried helping and look where that had gotten her. The best thing she could do was keep her mouth shut . . . and her lust contained.

"Well, let's get started." She headed to the tables where she and Jesse had placed the sign. Last night, she had primed and painted over the original sign so it was now a blank slate.

When Reid saw it, he wasn't too happy. "I thought we were just going to paint over the extra *t*."

That would have been much simpler, but she felt like she owed Noelle and Sheryl Ann more than just a simple paint job. "The sign was old and needed repainting anyway. So I decided to completely redo it."

She had let Noelle believe she was just helping Sophie out, but she would find out eventually—along with all the other sisters—that Sunny was actually the one responsible for both times the sign had been defaced. Sunny was sure the gossip was already spreading like wildfire. That's why she wanted to make the sign spectacular. She hoped it would be a small way to show everyone how sorry she was.

Collecting her supplies, she got to work applying the stencils she'd made for the lettering and sketching out the graphics. Since Noelle now made all kinds of desserts, not just muffins, Sunny had decided to fill the sign with pies, cupcakes, cookies, and other delicious treats.

She was so focused on sketching the perfect graphics she didn't notice Reid standing behind her watching until he spoke.

"You're really good at that."

She jumped and dropped the pencil. When she turned to him, he was looking at the pie she'd just drawn.

"So where did you learn to do that? Or does it just come naturally?"

She went back to sketching. "A little of both. I've always had a knack for drawing, but I've also taken a lot of art classes."

There was a long pause before he spoke again. "I'm no artist, but I could probably stay between the lines of those lettering stencils.

It turned out he was much better at detail work than Sunny. As he painted each stenciled letter, he kept a steady hand and an intense focus that never strayed from his brush.

Sunny wasn't staying as focused. Every few seconds, she couldn't keep her gaze from wandering over to Reid. The sexy curve of his jeaned butt as he bent over the sign. The flexing of his forearm muscles with each stroke of his brush. The cute way the tip of his tongue peeked out between his lips as he concentrated on his task. She wondered if he gave the same intense focus to everything he did: herding cows, riding horses . . . making love.

The last thought conjured up other thoughts. Thoughts of Sunny being stretched out on the table while Reid completely focused on painting her—not with a paintbrush, but with his calloused fingertips, firm lips, and hot tongue.

"Am I doing it wrong?"

The words had her blinking out of her fantasy to see Reid glancing over at her with a questioning look.

"Umm . . . no, you're doing great." She turned back to the cupcake with sprinkles she'd been painting.

Once Reid finished painting all the letters he could paint without getting in Sunny's way, he took the brush to the sink to rinse it. With him gone, it was much easier to stay focused. In fact, she got so focused on her vision for the sign that she didn't pay much attention to what Reid was doing until he spoke.

"Did you paint this?"

She glanced up to see him standing at the easel in the corner, holding up the drop cloth.

"Don't look at that!" She quickly set down her paintbrush and hurried over to snatch the drop cloth out of his hand and re-cover the painting. His stunned look at her outburst had her face burning with embarrassment. "I'm sorry, but I don't want anyone to see something that was just for practice."

He glanced at the drop cloth. "It looks like you spent an awful lot of time on something that was just for practice." He looked back at her and his eyes narrowed. "So what's really going on?"

"I told you. I'm just protective about my art."

"So protective that you keep it covered with drop cloths and hide most of it in a storage unit in Houston, instead of using it to fill your brand-new gallery?"

Sunny stared at him. "How do you know that?"

"Sophie told me. I wanted to know exactly what you had talked about at Cooper Springs so there wouldn't be any more surprises." He studied her with those intense amber eyes. "So what's the deal? Why are you hiding all your paintings?"

She could have lied, but it seemed useless now. Soon the entire town would know that she was not only a devious prankster, but also a fraud. Reid might as well be one of the firsts.

"Because all I can paint is angry art."

His brow knitted. "Angry art? Why do you call it that?"

"Because I only seem to be able to paint when I'm angry or upset."

"And how often is that?"

She swallowed hard. "A lot more than anyone would think."

He studied her for a long time before he spoke. "Does it work? I've been pretty angry myself lately. Maybe I should take it up." He glanced at Sophie sleeping on the bed. "Instead of taking my anger out on an innocent kid because my life didn't go the way I thought it would."

"Join the club. I didn't exactly plan to be an artist with a gallery she can't fill."

He glanced back at her. "So fill it."

"With what?"

He waved a hand at the easel. "Angry art."

"Are you crazy? I can't show that?"

"Why not? I realize that I show too much anger, but maybe you don't show enough. It's okay for people to get angry, Sunny. Just because your name is Sunshine, you don't always have to be smiling."

"I know that."

He raised his eyebrows. "Do you?" He lifted a hand and brushed a finger over her cheek. It was like he'd painted her with fire. She'd done a lot of thrill-seeking things in her life, but not one had made her tummy drop like Reid's touch.

"Paint," he said. But his hand didn't drop after he brushed off her cheek. Instead, his fingers curled behind her chin as his gaze lowered to her lips. "Sometimes," he said in a low whisper. "You just have to give in to your emotions." His thumb slowly stroked her bottom lip. "Or it makes you crazy."

He dipped his head and his lips replaced his thumb. It wasn't a devouring kiss like he'd given her in front of the sheriff's office. This kiss was soft and gentle. And yet, it wrecked her just as much.

Maybe more.

She could tell by the tremble in his fingers cradling her jaw that he was holding his passion on a short leash—no doubt because Sophie slept only feet away. The fact that he wanted her so badly was a major aphrodisiac. When he swiped his tongue over her bottom lip before he gave it a gentle nip, she couldn't help but release a soft moan.

"Shh . . ." His breath fell against her lips before

he deepened the kiss, his lips molding to hers as his tongue swept into her mouth.

She tried to move closer, needing to feel the hard press of his muscles, but his hand closed around her hip and firmly held her away. Even that turned her on. Which made no sense. She had never liked being controlled. But with Reid, she liked it. She liked it a lot. Mixed in with the lust was the same feeling she'd felt the night he'd pushed her behind the rock and covered her with his body. A feeling of contentment and security.

She would have continued to kiss him all day if they hadn't been interrupted by a loud tapping.

They jumped apart and turned to the bed, but Sophie was still sleeping soundly. The tapping came again and Sunny realized it was coming from the window. She was more than a little surprised to see a gray parrot sitting on the ledge. A gray parrot that stared straight at Sunny with its beady eyes before squawking.

"Bullshit!"

Chapter Thirteen

"WHAT DO YOU mean you're not going to come get it?" Sunny glanced at the bird perched on the top edge of her angry art. It stared back with a mean look.

"Bullshit!"

She couldn't really argue with the bird. This was bullshit. And all her fault. She shouldn't have opened the window and let the cussing parrot fly in. Of course, she'd made a lot of mistakes today . . . including kissing Reid when she'd vowed to avoid him.

"Sorry, honey," Melba said. "But birds aren't really my specialty. And if you and Reid couldn't catch it, I doubt I can. But I can call my friend at the Austin animal humane shelter and see if he knows of someone who could come get Jimmy Buffett."

"Jimmy Buffett?"

"You have to give the poor thing a name and I think it's fitting, don't you? And until someone can get there, you might want to get a cage. If you place his food and water in it, he'll probably fly right in."

Sunny sighed. "Fine. But I'd appreciate it if you'd call your friend as soon as possible." Once she'd hung up, she turned to Reid who was standing there with a smug smile on his face. "You think this is funny?"

"You have to admit it's a little funny." His smile got even bigger. "Jimmy Buffett?"

"You know Melba and her names."

"Who's Jimmy Buffet?" Sophie asked. She had roused from her nap during the chaotic bird chase and was now sitting on the bed, cuddling Patsy, who was watching the parrot as skeptically as Sophie. "Do parrots eat rabbits?"

"No," Reid said. "I've concluded from all the food I've put out for him that he loves sweet potatoes and apples, but hates lettuce and blueberries." He glanced at Sunny. "So I'd steer clear of those."

She shook her head. "Oh, no. I'm not keeping him. Y'all are taking him with you as soon as we catch him in a cage." She tapped her phone and pulled up Amazon to order one. "After all, you were the one he followed here. Probably because you've become his main food source."

"Sorry, but you're the one who let him in. Besides, I already have a rabbit . . . and a teenager." He glanced at Sophie. "You feeling up to finishing the sign, Soph?"

Sophie turned out to be an enthusiastic, if not a little sloppy, painter. She wielded a paintbrush like it was a wizardry wand and she was Hermione trying to save Harry. But Sunny had never believed in stifling people's creativity so she kept her thoughts to herself . . . and a rag at the ready. When Sophie ended up being so thrilled with the finished product, Sunny was glad she'd given the teenager free rein.

"It looks awesome!" Sophie exclaimed as they all three stared down at the swirling black letters intermingled with tempting baked goods.

"Awesome, shithead!" Jimmy Buffett squawked from his perch on the angry art.

Reid rolled his eyes at the bird as he draped an arm over his niece's shoulders. "You're right, Soph. We did do a good job, didn't we? I wonder if I should become a painter instead of a rancher."

"Stick with ranching," Sunny said. "Believe me, it's much more lucrative."

Reid studied her over Sophie's head. "Maybe it's not about money. Maybe it's just about doing what you love."

There had been a time when Sunny hadn't cared about making money on her art. She'd just loved doing it. But somewhere along the way, she'd lost that love. It wasn't so much about the money as much as it was about people liking her work . . . liking her.

That's what it boiled down to.

She was her art. If people and critics didn't like it, they didn't like her.

The clatter of multiple heels pulled Sunny from her thoughts and she turned to the stairs. She hoped it was Melba and her friend coming for the parrot. She wasn't that lucky. Talk about the fear of people not liking her. That fear swelled to overflowing as all six members of the Secret Sisterhood stepped into the attic.

She knew why the Holiday sisters were there.

They were there to kick a lying prankster out of their club. Thankfully, they were distracted from their mission by Jimmy Buffett.

"Where did that parrot come from?" Liberty stared at the bird in confusion.

Hallie looked at Reid. "Is that the parrot you've been telling me about? I see you finally got it down from the tree."

"He followed me from the ranch." He flashed a smirk at Sunny. "And apparently took a liking to the Sunshine Room. He flew right in when Sunny opened the window."

"Don't worry, Libby," Sunny said. "Jimmy Buffett isn't staying. Melba is sending someone to get him."

"I don't care if he stays." Liberty stepped closer to the bird. "He's kinda cute."

"Bullshit!"

Liberty jumped back at Jimmy's outburst. "Or not."

All the sisters laughed before Noelle noticed the sign.

"Is that the sign? Oh my gosh! I love it! It's just perfect. It keeps the beloved name, but also says at one glance that we offer much more than just muffins." She looked at Sophie and winked. "Of course, it would be much funnier with an extra *t*."

Sophie blushed. "I'm so sorry, Ms. Remington.

I don't know what got into me. If there's anything I can do to make it up to you, I swear I will."

"The sign is certainly a start. But I could also use some help at the bakery."

Sophie's eyes widened with excitement. "You want me to work at the bakery?"

"Just for a few hours after school." Noelle glanced at Reid. "If that's okay with you, Reid."

"As long as it doesn't interfere with her schoolwork."

"It won't, Uncle Reid." Sophie bounced on her toes. "I promise. I also promise to get my chores done and take care of Patsy."

"Then it's fine with me." Reid looked at Noelle. "Do you need her today?"

"Monday will be soon enough for her to start."

"She'll be there." Reid turned to Sophie who was busting with happiness. "Come on, Soph, let's let these ladies enjoy the rest of their afternoon together while we go get some tacos. I'm starving." He hesitated. "You want to drive?"

Sophie released a squeal and quickly collected her sneakers and Patsy while Reid changed out of his paint shirt. Sunny wished she could leave with them. But her days of avoiding things were over. Once Reid and Sophie were gone, all the sisters turned to her and there was nothing to do but face the music.

She swallowed hard. "I know why y'all are here. And I don't blame you. I deserve to be kicked out of the Secret Sisterhood."

"Kicked out?" Belle stared at her. "Why would you think we came to kick you out?"

"Because I'm a horrible person who sneaks around vandalizing the town."

Liberty snorted. "You were a teenager, Sunny. We all pull stunts as teenagers."

"But I didn't tell y'all. And the main rule of the Sisterhood is never keep secrets from sisters."

"True," Sweetie said. "But it's not like all of us haven't kept secrets from each other before. I didn't tell anyone how unhappy I was in Nashville."

"And I didn't tell y'all about my plan to marry Rome and save the ranch until after the fact," Cloe added.

Liberty rubbed her rounded belly. "I failed to mention how upset I was when I thought I couldn't have kids."

"I didn't tell anyone about pulling the twin switch." Belle glanced at Hallie and waited.

Hallie huffed. "Fine! I didn't tell anyone about having a one-night stand with Jace. But Noelle was the biggest liar because she kept acting like she hated Casey when she really . . . lo-o-oves him."

Noelle laughed. "I did, didn't I?" She glanced at Sunny and her laughter faded. "The point is that we've all kept our secrets, Sunny. So we're not going to throw you out of the club for yours. If anyone should be thrown out of the club, it should be me." Her eyes glittered with tears. "Your high school pranks got me to thinking and I realized that . . . I'm a mean girl."

Sunny stared at her best friend. "What? You

don't have a mean bone in your body, Noelle Holiday Remington."

"I didn't think I did, but it's pretty mean to not welcome the new girl in school with open arms."

"You did welcome me, Elle. You showed me around the school that first day and were always nice to me when we saw each other in the halls."

"I was nice, but I should have included you in things much more than I did. I was so caught up in my feud with Casey, I didn't make you feel like you were part of this town. And I'm sorry, Sunny." Tears dripped down her cheeks. "I'm so, so sorry."

"Oh, Elle!" Sunny pulled her into a tight hug. "There's no need to apologize. It's all just water under the bridge." But as she said the words, she realized that what had happened in high school hadn't been water under the bridge . . . until now. Noelle's acknowledgement and apology had lifted the darkness from the past by shining a light on it. She drew back and looked at her friend. "Okay, maybe you should have been more welcoming. But I should have made more of an effort too, instead of acting like I was just fine and dandy spending time alone drawing in my sketchpad." She hesitated. "I'm good at hiding my true emotions."

"Well, I think we need to make a new pact," Sweetie said. "No more keeping secrets from sisters." She held out her hand and the other sisters placed theirs on top of hers.

Everyone but Sunny.

When they all looked at her, she blurted out the truth. "I can't paint!"

All the sisters lowered their hands and stared at her with confusion.

"What do you mean you can't paint?" Belle asked. "We all have paintings in our houses that you've painted for us, Sunny. Corbin and I have at least five."

"Those were all done months and months ago, before I got painter's block. I haven't done anything worth putting into a gallery for close to a year."

Liberty glanced at the covered painting Jimmy Buffett was still perched on. "What about that one?"

Sunny shook her head. "That's not art. It's just me flinging paint in frustration."

"Aww, Sunny." Belle took her hand and squeezed it. "Why didn't you say anything?"

Sunny sighed. "Because I didn't want to disappoint y'all. But I should have said something . . . especially before Corbin built me a gallery."

Belle gave her a soft smile. "Corbin doesn't care about a silly gallery. He cares about you. He's been worried sick since learning about the pranks you pulled on the townsfolk."

Sunny's heart sank. "He must think I'm the biggest disappointment of his life."

"I don't think that's how he feels at all." Belle squeezed her hand. "But there's only one way to find out. He's downstairs waiting to talk to you."

The last thing Sunny wanted to do was face her

brother. But she knew she would have to eventually. It might as well be now.

She found him out back playing catch with Buck Owens and Mickey Gilley. She would have thought the long-legged poodle mix would beat out the fat pug for the ball every time. But Gilley seemed to enjoy the chase more than the ball. He ran loops around Buck, then barked excitedly when the pug grabbed the ball in his mouth.

Sunny stood by the back door and watched until Corbin glanced up and saw her. In his eyes, there was no disappointment. Just love. He dropped the ball and held out his arms. She didn't hesitate to walk straight into them and bury her face against his chest, like she had done countless times in her life.

"I guess you're here to figure out why your sister is such a mess."

Corbin held her tight. "You're not a mess. You were just a young teenage girl trying to survive the crazy life she was born into."

She drew back. "You had the same life, Cory, and you didn't pull stupid pranks."

"No. Instead I became an angry young man with a huge chip on my shoulder. We both dealt with our pain the only way we knew how." He hesitated. "But I wish you would have told me how you were feeling, Sunny."

"You already had too much to deal with. I didn't want you to have to worry about me too."

"But that's my job . . . taking care of you."

This wasn't the first time Corbin had spoken the words, but it was the first time Sunny had actually heard them. Before they had just been words repeated so many times that they'd become interwoven into her psyche. Corbin took care of her. He'd always taken care of her. That was his job.

Except it had never been his job. It had been their parents' job. Parents took care of their children until their children were old enough to take care of themselves. But Corbin and Sunny had never had a normal childhood so they'd clung to the only thing that felt normal.

Corbin taking care of Sunny and Sunny letting him.

That didn't make it right.

"It's not your job to take care of me, Cory," she said. "It's time I took care of myself."

"And you're going to do that just as soon as you get your gallery up and running."

She shook her head. "I'm not going to get the gallery up and running. I'm not an artist worthy of having her own gallery."

He stared at her. "What are you talking about? You're a great artist."

"I've never been a great artist. I'm mediocre at best. Certainly not good enough to support myself with my art."

"But what about all the paintings you've sold at your art showings?"

"I lied. All those paintings are in a storage unit in Houston. And I'm sorry, Cory. I'm so sorry for lying to you. I'll figure out a way to pay you back for all the money you spent renovating the gallery."

"I don't care about the money, Sunny. I care about you. You don't have to sell a single painting as far as I'm concerned. I just want you to do what makes you happy."

That was the problem. She had spent so much time worrying about making Corbin and other people happy that she hadn't thought about what would make her happy.

"What if I don't know what will make me happy?"

He pulled her into his arms. "Then we'll figure it out together. No more hiding how you feel."

"Even if I'm not your happy-go-lucky sister?"

He leaned back and tweaked her nose. "Even then. You loved me when I was grumpy. I figure I can love you when you are." He hesitated and an evil twinkle entered his eyes. "Although I have the secret weapon against grumpiness." He held up his hands and wiggled his fingers. "The Tickle Monster."

She tried to run, but he easily caught her and tickled her until she shrieked with laughter. When he finally stopped, he leaned down and picked up something from the ground. It was Mrs. Fields's letter. It must have fallen out of her pocket.

Corbin waved it at her with a grin. "What's this? Are you getting love letters from some guy in town?"

"Not hardly. It's one of the letters Jesse found in a trunk when he was renovating my room. I guess Mrs. Fields saved all the letters her admirers sent her, although that one isn't admiring as much as threatening. Have you ever heard of someone living in town with the initials U.T.?"

Surprise registered on Corbin's face and he quickly opened the letter and started reading it. His brow furrowed. When Corbin furrowed his brow, something wasn't right.

"What is it, Cory?"

He finished reading the letter before he glanced up. "Remember the bet I made with Mrs. Stokes about her quitting smoking? Well, it wasn't really a bet. It was more a deal. If she quit smoking, I'd look into a strange letter she found in her father's things. The letter was from Mrs. Fields stating that the problem had been taken care of."

"What problem?"

"I don't know and neither does Fiona Stokes."

"And you think this letter and that letter are connected? Maybe it was a completely different problem."

Corbin shook his head. "Doubtful when Mrs. Stokes's father's name was Ulysses Thompson."

Chapter Fourteen

"Do you think I could get my own horse one day?"

Reid glanced over at Sophie. Two weeks ago, she'd been terrified to even come near a horse. Which explained why she had refused to help out at the ranch. Now she sat a saddle almost as well as he did and loved being at the ranch. Not only because she loved to ride, but also because the Holidays spoiled her rotten.

If Hank and Hallie weren't teaching her how to rope, Darla was teaching her how to cook or Mimi was teaching her how to garden and sew. When she wasn't at the ranch with him, she was at Nothin' But Muffins with Noelle learning to bake or doing community service for the entire town, learning to be responsible.

Sophie was thriving under all the attention. While she still could be moody, she talked and laughed now. She had stopped wearing as much makeup—thanks to Sunny taking her makeup shopping and having the saleswoman give her a few tips—and, yesterday, she'd been greeted by a group of girls when he dropped her off at school.

Her drastic change made him realize what a pigheaded fool he'd been. If he hadn't been so stubborn and accepted help sooner, Sophie would have been happier much sooner. He wanted to continue to make her happy, but he refused to lie to accomplish it.

"I'm sorry, Soph, but we don't have the money for a horse."

"But maybe one day? When you get your own ranch?"

He glanced over at her with surprise. "How did you know I wanted my own ranch?"

"Mama told me. She said you talked about having your own ranch nonstop when you were a kid."

Memories of his childhood with Bree still made him sad, but now mixed with that sadness was a nostalgic, bittersweet feeling. He figured that was progress.

"That I did," he said with a soft smile. "I talked on and on about my ranch while your mama talked nonstop about opening her own hair salon."

Sophie stared at him. "She did? But she was horrible with hair. She couldn't get my hair into a smooth ponytail to save her soul. And she was always dyeing her hair weird colors."

He laughed. "I remember that. She once tried to give me blond highlights and I ended up with red-striped hair. Although all my second-grade friends thought it was cool."

Sophie giggled. "I would have liked to see that. But, unlike Mama with hair, you're good at ranching." Her smile faded. "Me and Mama ruined your ranch dream, didn't we? That's why you were so mad at me."

He started to deny it, but then realized Sophie was too smart for that. "I did blame you and your mama, but the truth is that y'all weren't to blame for me not getting a ranch. I didn't have nearly enough money saved up to buy a ranch and probably never would have. And that's okay because everything turned out in the long run. I'm doing what I love to do." He winked at her. "And now I get it to do it with my niece."

"But this ranch isn't yours."

"True, but neither are all the headaches and bills."

She smiled sadly. "Mama hated paying bills. Which probably explained why we kept getting kicked out of our apartments. The longest we stayed in one place was after you showed up."

He struggled with how to reply without casting a bad light on Bree. "Your mama was a free spirit. She liked going wherever the wind blew her."

"It blew her a lot. I don't like being blown around." She glanced over at him. "I like staying in one place."

He knew she wasn't just making small talk. She was asking for something. Something he was going to try his damnedest to give her. "Okay then. We'll stay put for a while."

"But what if you lose your job here? Mama had trouble keeping jobs."

The question broke his heart. "I'm not your

mama, Soph. I'm not going to do anything to lose my job. And I'll make sure you don't have to change schools again until you head to college."

"You'd do that for me?"

"I'm not just doing it for you, Soph. I like staying in one place too."

She smiled. "I guess we're two peas in a pod."

He smiled back. "I guess we are."

A sassy sparkle entered her eyes. "Race you back to the house!" She took off at full gallop.

He easily caught up with her and pulled ahead. No one liked to win if they thought people let them. But when the barn came into view, he eased back just enough to let her horse beat his by a nose. It was worth the bright smile she flashed when they reached the barn.

"I won!"

"You sure did!" Mimi called from the porch. "I witnessed it with my own two eyes. Now y'all come and get some egg salad sandwiches and sweet tea."

Sophie didn't have to be asked twice. She was headed for the porch before Reid could even dismount. After he took care of the horses, he followed.

The Holidays' porch was always decorated for the upcoming holiday. Darla Holiday loved holidays, which was why she had named all her daughters after the holiday their birthdays fell on or around. Something Reid hadn't figured out until Jace had called Hallie by her given name, Halloween, and all hell had broken loose. In February, the porch had been covered with hearts and cupids. In March, shamrocks and leprechauns. Now, it was decorated for Easter with a flowered wreath on the door, ceramic bunnies and chicks lining the windowsills, and a basket of dyed colored eggs sitting in the center of the table Sophie and Mimi were sitting at . . . and Corbin.

Reid didn't know when Corbin had joined the lunch party, but he wasn't too happy about it. He'd always been uncomfortable around his head boss. After kissing Sunny twice, Reid was even more so. He quickly made up an excuse for why he couldn't stay.

"Thanks for the lunch invite, Ms. Mimi, but I need to go check in with Hallie. We're suppose to move the south herd to get them ready for branding."

"That will have to wait until tomorrow," Mimi said. "Hallie's a little off her feed today."

"Is she okay?"

A smile stretched across Mimi's face. "Right as rain. Now come take a seat, Reid. I already made you a plate." She stood. "I'm gonna go make some more iced tea."

With no other choice, besides being rude, Reid took off his hat and climbed the steps. Corbin and Sophie seemed to be in deep conversation about something. Reid didn't pay much attention to what they were saying until he'd taken a seat and picked up his sandwich.

". . . I still don't get it, Corbin," Sophie said. "What did your mama and daddy's fighting have to do with anything?"

Reid's eyes widened and he quickly swallowed

the bite of sandwich he'd just taken. "I don't think you should be asking such personal questions, Soph."

"That's okay," Corbin said. "It's a good question. One I'm not sure I have a good answer for."

Sophie picked up a potato chip and munched it. "My mama told me she got in a lot of fights with my daddy before he ran off, but that didn't make her get rid of me." Before Reid could get after Sophie for giving out too much information, Corbin cut him off.

"And that's how it should be. Parents shouldn't get rid of their kids just because they can't live with their significant other. Although I think my and Sunny's parents just used their fights as an excuse to pawn us off on relatives."

"But that's just plain child abuse," Sophie said. "Especially when Mimi told me your Uncle Dan was a good-for-nothin' drunk."

Reid choked. "Soph!"

Corbin laughed. "She's just stating the truth. Uncle Dan was a good-for-nothing drunk and pawning your kids off on any relative that would take them is child abuse. But Sunny and I survived."

"Thanks to you," Sophie said. "Sunny told me about how you took care of her and worked to make sure she could have brand-name athletic shoes like the other kids at school."

Reid felt more than a little stunned. While he was digesting everything he'd just learned, the screen door opened and Mimi came out carrying a pitcher of iced tea. She set it on the table before she glanced at Sophie. "Darla and I are getting ready to make some blueberry pies. You want to help?"

Sophie jumped up. "Of course I do!"

Once the screen door slammed behind her and Mimi, Corbin smiled at Reid. "She's really come out of her shell."

"I'm sorry if she got too personal."

"She didn't. Everyone in town knows about my and Sunny's upbringing. Although by the stunned look on your face, I'd say that you didn't."

Reid shook his head. "No, sir." He'd assumed the Whitlocks had grown up with silver spoons in their mouths. Finding out that they hadn't left him feeling more than a little broadsided and speechless.

"I guess that's where the old adage 'never judge a book by its cover' comes from," Corbin said. "Although I can see where you'd get the idea. Sunny plays a spoiled little rich girl well."

She had played it well. She had certainly fooled Reid. Just like she had fooled everyone into believing she was just a happy-go-lucky woman without a care in the world. Her angry art said differently. Reid couldn't help wondering if Corbin knew about the art. He doubted it. It seemed Sunny Whitlock had become extremely good at hiding her true feelings. He had to wonder if that's how she'd dealt with her parents' abuse.

"Are you interested in my sister?"

Corbin's question brought Reid out of his

thoughts. He stared at his boss, thinking he'd misunderstood. "Excuse me, sir?"

"Sunny. Are you interested in her?"

He scrambled for a reply that wouldn't be a boldfaced lie, and also wouldn't get him fired, and came up empty. After the kiss in Sunny's attic room, there was little doubt that he was interested in her. More than interested. She had a hold on him that went way beyond mere interest. It was bordering on complete infatuation. He spent his nights dreaming about her and his days trying to push thoughts of her out of his head—unsuccessfully. Now he was going to get fired because he couldn't control his obsession with her. But he wouldn't go down without a fight. He owed Sophie that much.

"I guess Mrs. Stokes told you about what happened in town. And I want to apologize, sir. I totally overstep my bounds. I promise it won't happen again."

Corbin's eyebrows lifted. "Exactly what happened in town?"

Reid cringed. Shit. He walked right into that one. With no way out, he told the truth. "I kissed your sister. But it just . . . sorta happened."

"Ahh." Corbin didn't look surprised at all. "So that explains why Mrs. Stokes thinks you're interested in Sunny. And I must admit, I was kind of hoping you were. Sunny could use a stable man like you in her life." Reid felt like his jaw hit the table as Corbin continued. "And just so you know, I would never fire you over a kiss . . . unless it was forced."

"No, sir. It wasn't forced. She . . . it wasn't forced."

Corbin smiled. "I understand. Sunny can be hard to say no to. I'm certainly not good at doing it. I've spoiled her rotten, which probably explains why she's so flighty."

"I wouldn't say she's flighty."

Corbin tipped his head. "You wouldn't? How would you describe my sister?"

Reid thought for only a moment before he answered. "Sunny's like a beam of sunlight. You can't keep a beam of sunlight in one place and you shouldn't expect to. It has to constantly move with the positioning of the sun. But while it's shining on you, you feel warm and grateful." Once the words were out, he didn't know who was more surprised by them—he or Corbin.

A beam of sunlight? Where had that come from?

But it was the truth. Sunny had certainly been a beam of sunlight for Reid. She'd shed light on the mistakes he was making with Sophie and helped him to become a better guardian. A better person. Now, he realized it was because she had walked in Sophie's shoes and knew what it was like to be dumped off on an inept relative. While most people became angry and jaded after enduring such a horrible childhood, Sunny kept smiling and spreading her light—only showing her pain and anger through her art.

That bothered Reid more than he cared to admit. He might have showed his anger too much, but hiding it wasn't good either. He was on the verge of mentioning the angry art to Corbin when the screen door flew open and Hallie strode out to the porch.

She didn't look sick. Just annoyed.

"Come on, Reid. We need to head out to the west pasture and check the fences. Decker called and said someone spotted cows wandering along the highway and I'm worried they're ours. Plus if I stay around my overprotective mama and know-it-all grandma for one more second, I might scream."

Reid jumped up. "Yes, ma'am." He grabbed the other half of his sandwich to eat on the way. It was a bad idea. A glop of egg salad fell out and landed on Hallie's boot. She took one look at the egg and mayo mixture and her face lost all color. Covering her mouth, she whirled and pushed past Mimi who was just coming out the door.

Mimi smiled slyly as she watched her granddaughter disappear inside the house. "I know what I know." She looked at Reid. "And I know you're going to need to take care of those cows and fences by yourself."

Chapter Fifteen

Reid spent the rest of the day searching for stray cows and fixing fences in the west pasture. With the temperatures in the mid-eighties, by quitting time, he felt like a sweat-soaked, wrung-out dishrag. On the way to the trailer, he called Sophie to see if she wanted to go to Cooper Springs for a swim.

"Do I have to, Uncle Reid? I'm helping Mimi plant her vegetable garden and Darla asked if I could stay for supper. She said you're welcome too. We're going to have tuna casserole and one of the blueberry pies I helped her make for dessert."

"That sounds delicious, but I'm pretty beat. I'm just going to take a quick swim and go back to the trailer. But that doesn't mean you can't stay. Just make sure you thank the Holidays for the invite and call me when you're ready for me to come pick you up. I don't want you walking home in the dark."

"Yes, sir."

It was the first time she'd called him *sir* and he was a little taken back. "Umm . . . okay then. Have fun."

When he got to the trailer, he let Patsy Cline out of her enclosure in Sophie's room to get some exercise while he changed into his swim trunks. For only having three legs, the rabbit was fast and agile. She had made herself an obstacle course through the house that included racing down the hallway, across his bed, then racing back down the hallway to dive over the living room ottoman before heading to Sophie's room. He let her do the circuit over and over again until she wore herself out, then he scooped her up and put her back in her enclosure. Once he filled her food and water bowls, he grabbed a towel and headed out.

After his long, sweaty day, the cold water felt like heaven. He swam a little, then floated on his back and watched the sunset lower behind the tree line as his thoughts drifted to the last time he'd been there.

That night, he'd been such an arrogant jerk to Sunny. He'd convinced himself that his rejection of her had to do with her being Corbin's sister and him not wanting to get fired. And that had been some of it. But most of it had been jealousy—jealousy that she had everything handed to her on a silver platter while he'd had all his dreams taken away.

But she hadn't had things handed to her on a silver platter. Her life had been so much worse than his. And yet, she had never let her childhood, or her inability to succeed at what she loved, make her resentful and angry. Unlike him, she didn't focus on the tragedies in her life. Instead, she pinned a smile on her face and focused on being happy.

His assessment of her was right. She was a sunbeam. A bright sunbeam that made people feel warm and happy. He'd certainly become happier since she'd arrived. But that didn't mean he should be obsessing about her. Corbin might say he didn't mind Reid dating her, but Reid wasn't about to go down that treacherous road. Relationships were hard enough for normal folks who didn't have a lot of psychological baggage. Between her parents and his father, he and Sunny needed a damn aircraft carrier for their baggage.

Yes, he wanted her. He had never wanted a woman more. And yes, he liked her. He liked her a lot. But he had made a vow to Sophie to keep this job and dating Sunny was a surefire way to screw that up. Reid didn't exactly have a good record with relationships. In fact, he had no record. He didn't know what a woman needed to be happy. Hell, he was just figuring out what made him happy.

No, Sunny was not for him. Period.

"Reid?"

He came up out of his float as if a shark had suddenly appeared. But it wasn't a shark standing on the shore with the setting sun reflecting off her hair in rivers of golds and reds. It was Sunny. Sunny in the same yellow sundress she'd worn at her surprise birthday party, the pink-painted toes of her bare feet standing out like tiny flowers against the muddy brown of the shore.

In the last couple weeks, he'd only seen her

briefly when he dropped Sophie off for community service. Every time, he felt like he was walking a tightrope of desire. And that had been with Sophie there. Now that they were alone, that tightrope felt even more slippery and dangerous. Or maybe what made it more slippery and dangerous was that another layer of her façade had been peeled back.

He no longer saw a spoiled little rich girl.

He saw a strong woman who had survived a horrible childhood the only way she knew how.

"I'm not stalking you if that's what you're thinking. Mimi called and told me the sisters were meeting here for a swim." She glanced around. "Has anyone shown up?"

"No, but I'm sure they'll be here soon."

He swam to shore. He had no desire to be part of the Holiday sisters' swimming party. Or to be alone with Sunny. But when he stepped out of the springs, he didn't grab his towel and hurry to leave. He just stood there . . . basking in Sunshine.

She did shine. He struggled to take his gaze off the wealth of sunlit hair that fell around her bare shoulders and the full curves of her breasts. He remembered those sweet breasts well. Every night, he fantasized about filling his hands to overflowing with their abundant flesh before taking their centers into his mouth and suckling until they pebbled hard and needy against his tongue.

Her gaze ran over him as well.

He had never been one to think too much about his body. He fed it when it was hungry and gave it rest when it was tired. But he didn't worry about what women thought of it . . . until now. He wanted Sunny to like what she saw and he couldn't help flexing the muscles hard ranch work had given him.

After a thorough perusal, her brown-eyed gaze lifted and locked with his. There was a long silence that should have been awkward but wasn't.

Leave now, his brain said. But his body refused to listen.

"Sophie's really enjoying community service," he said.

A soft smile lifted the corners of her mouth. "I am too." She leaned down and picked up the towel he'd left on a rock and held it out. "You have goose bumps."

Those goose bumps increased when he took the towel and their fingers brushed. He quickly started drying off, grasping for any safe topic. "I guess Melba never came and got Jimmy Buffet. Sophie mentioned you still have him."

"No. She says she doesn't do birds."

"So you're keeping him?"

"Not forever." She pulled her cellphone out of a bag at her feet. "But since I already invested in a cage, water bottle, and toys, I told her I would keep him until she could find someone to take him."

"So he's caged now?"

She glanced up from the cellphone she'd been tapping on—no doubt texting the Holiday sisters to see where they were. "Are you kidding? He only flies into it after I fall asleep. And only to eat and throw his birdseed onto the floor. The rest of the time, he sits on my easel and yells cusswords at me while I paint."

He laughed, but then quickly sobered when her words registered. "You've been angry?"

Her cheeks flushed and she looked away. "No. Not angry art. Once everyone saw the Nothin' But Muffins sign, they put in requests with the town council for me to paint new signs for them as part of my community service."

"And here you thought no one liked your paintings." He was teasing her, but when he saw her sad expression, he realized his teasing had fallen short.

"Yeah, I'm great at painting cupcakes, barbecue ribs, and tacos."

"Hey, very few people can paint food as well as you do." He hesitated. "I guess you haven't been able to paint anything else."

She shook her head. "And I've given up trying." She hesitated. "I found a job in Dallas doing web design."

He didn't know why he felt like she had just slapped him hard across the face. "You're leaving?"

She nodded, refusing to look at him. "But I'd appreciate it if you didn't say anything to anyone until I've told my family."

He stood there staring at her as an incoming text pinged her phone. She was leaving. Sunny was leaving. He should be jumping up and down with joy. Once she was gone, he could finally get on with his life and stop obsessing about her. Out of sight, out of mind. But it wasn't joy that sat at the bottom of his stomach like a lump of coal.

"That's weird." She glanced up from her phone. "According to Noelle, there's no Secret Sisterhood skinny-dipping party tonight."

"Secret Sisterhood skinny-dipping party?"

Her pretty brown eyes widened. "Oops. That's supposed to be a secret. Can you just forget you heard that?"

It was doubtful he'd ever forget the thought of seven beautiful women swimming naked. Or maybe it was just this beautiful woman swimming naked that he'd never forget.

And she was leaving.

He'd never again see her brilliant smile or hear her wind-chiming laughter or smell her lemony scent ... or kiss her warm, sweet lips that had held nothing back from him.

"I don't think you should leave." The words just popped out, surprising him as much as they seemed to surprise her.

She tipped her head. "Why?"

He scrambled for a reason that didn't involve the giant lump of coal in the pit of his stomach. "Because your family is here. And I've learned that family is important. I never realized how much until I lost my sister." He ran a hand through his wet hair and sighed. "I wasn't the best brother. I was too wrapped up in owning my own ranch to care about what she was going through. And I'll regret that every day for the rest of my life. I don't want you to make the same mistake. Everyone here loves you, Sunshine. And if I've learned anything since being here, it's that success isn't about owning a ranch ... or selling a bunch of paintings. It's about being loved."

He didn't know where the words came from, but he knew they were true. Love was much more important than ranches. And hurt feelings. He wished he'd figured that out before he'd cut off his sister for hurting his when she left home. He wished he'd tried harder to see her and Sophie. Tried harder to get them to come home. It wouldn't have changed her getting cancer, but it would have given them much more time together before she passed.

If he had a chance to make sure Sunny didn't make the same mistake, he was going to take it—even if he had to spend his days and nights obsessing about her. But before he could continue to persuade her, she did something he least expected.

She burst into tears.

Seeing sunshine turn to rain was the most heart-wrenching thing Reid had ever witnessed in his life. Especially when he was the one responsible.

He moved to take her in his arms, but she turned her back to him.

"I'm fine. Just fine. You can go. I just need a second. Alone."

Her words broke his heart even more. Like the angry art she kept hidden, she didn't want anyone to see her without a smile on her face. No doubt that was the reason she painted angry art. She desperately needed an outlet. Even though there was a mountain of reasons for why he should listen to her and walk away, he couldn't do it.

He wanted to be her outlet.

He wanted to be the one person she shared her true emotions with.

Ignoring her dismissal, he pulled her into his arms. She stiffened for only a moment before she melted against him and buried her tear-soaked face in his chest. He held her close, trying to absorb all her sadness.

"Take all the time you need, Sunshine. I'm not going anywhere."

As it turned out, she needed a lot of crying time. The sun had disappeared and a blanket of stars had replaced it when her sobs finally turned to soft hiccups. Still, he would have stood there holding her and rubbing her back until the sun rose again if that was what she needed.

"I'm sorry," she said in a nasally voice.

"There's no need to apologize for your true feelings, Sunny. You have every right to feel what you feel."

She sniffed. "So you're saying you enjoy women covering your chest with tears and snot?"

He laughed. "A little snot never hurt anyone." He drew back and lifted the towel he still held in his hand and blotted her tears from her cheeks. Her eyes were puffy and her lips held not even a hint of a smile. And yet, she had never looked more beautiful.

"Thank you," she whispered.

"I didn't do anything but give you a shoulder to cry on."

She lowered her gaze and her cheeks turned pink. "I don't usually cry on shoulders. I don't cry in front of people period."

He placed a finger under her chin and lifted her gaze back to his. "Then I'm glad you chose me to be the first."

The smile returned. Not a bright, flashy smile. This smile was soft and hesitant and made him feel like he was drowning and she was the only life preserver in sight. He didn't know how long they stood there staring at each other before her cellphone pinged.

She lifted the phone she still held and looked at the screen. "It's the rest of the sisters saying there was no skinny-dipping party tonight." She shook her head. "It doesn't make sense. Why would Mimi lie? What is that ornery woman up—" She cut off as her gaze snapped to him. "Did Mimi know you were coming here?"

"Not unless Sophie told her."

Sunny rolled her eyes and sighed. "Oh, Sophie told her. I don't doubt it for a second. Mimi is extremely good at throwing people together."

He cocked an eyebrow. "Throwing people together?"

"Matchmaking." She held up a hand. "And before you start pointing fingers at me, I had nothing to do with her matchmaking scheme. When she alluded to us getting together, I made it perfectly clear that you weren't interested in me."

He should have left it at that. But while he'd been holding her, he'd come to a realization. It didn't matter that she was his boss's little sister and he'd made a vow to Sophie to keep his job. Or that they had an aircraft carrier full of baggage, which might explain why neither one of them had ever had a serious relationship. None of those facts seemed to stop the feelings he had for this woman. And it was about time he stopped lying to himself.

And her.

"That's not exactly true," he said.

She looked at him with confusion. "Excuse me?"

He smoothed a strand of her hair, enjoying the silky feel of it slipping through his fingers as he tucked it behind the perfect shell of her ear. Just that mere touch had him trembling like a newborn calf taking its first steps. "The thing is . . . I *am* interested in you, Sunshine Whitlock. Extremely interested."

She blinked those big brown eyes. "But . . . what happened to me being trouble?"

"Oh, you're still trouble." He smiled. "But maybe it's time I got into a little trouble."

Chapter Sixteen

FOR THE FIRST time in her life, Sunny was speechless.

Sensible, responsible Reid Mitchell wanted to get into trouble . . . with her? It made no sense. No sense at all.

"W-W-Why?" she sputtered.

His calloused fingers slid along her jaw and lifted her chin until their gazes met. There was definite desire in his amber eyes. And something else. Something that made her heart beat faster as he spoke in a low raspy voice.

"Maybe I'm finally seeing the person behind the smile—the person you really are."

"The failing artist who is a liar, a vandal, and a horrible influence on innocent young girls?"

He shook his head. "No. The talented artist who struggles to believe in herself and puts everyone else's happiness above her own—even an innocent young girl's."

"I haven't made people very happy lately."

His eyes grew intense as he studied her. "It's not your responsibility to make everyone happy all the time, Sunshine. Sometimes, you just need to make yourself happy."

"That's the trouble. I don't know what will make me happy."

"Then I guess you'll just need to figure it out. Until then, hold your breath."

She stared at him. "What?"

"Hold your breath."

Before she had a chance to figure out what he was talking about, he scooped her into his arms and tossed her in the springs. The water was freezing and filled her nose when she sucked in from the shock of it. She surfaced, choking and trying to catch her breath as a strong arm wrapped around her waist and pulled her against a muscled chest.

"You okay? I told you to hold your breath."

She scraped her hair back and glared at the man grinning at her. "No one holds their breath when people tell them to. They're too busy thinking 'Why does he want me to hold my breath?' And the answer to that question, as far as you're concerned, wouldn't have been because you planned to toss me into the springs."

"And why not? You don't think I know how to have fun?"

"Actually, no."

He laughed. Since she was held tightly in his arms, she felt the husky rumble all the way down to her toes that were brushing against his hard calves.

"Okay," he said. "Fair enough. I haven't exactly been fun luvin'."

"Haven't exactly been?"

"Alright I haven't been. But I've decided to turn over a new leaf."

"And why is that?"

He studied her. "Maybe I'm taking a page from the Sunshine book and looking for the joy in life, instead of looking for the sorrow." He grinned a lecherous grin and easily lifted her high above his head.

"Don't you—"

That was all she got out before she went sailing through the air and landed in the water again. But this time she was more prepared. Instead of resurfacing, she stayed underwater and swam toward him. Since the bottom of the springs was lined with slippery moss and rock, it only took a tug to get his feet to slip out from under him. She tried to hold him under, but he was too strong. He pulled her to the surface in a tangle of arms and legs. He was laughing like crazy. She shoved her hair out of her face and scowled.

"I think I like the grumpy Gus better than the joking prankster."

"Says the woman who sent the mayor's underwear up the flagpole."

"I was a clueless teenager."

"So you're telling me you aren't interested in any more daredevil thrills?"

"That depends on what the thrill is."

His gaze lowered and his smile faded. She glanced down and realized that the ties on one side of her dress had come undone and her breast was almost completely bared.

She quickly went to cover it, but Reid encircled her wrist with his calloused fingers and stopped her. His amber gaze was intense and he looked hot, so hot, with his dark hair slicked back from his angular face like some kind of sexy magazine model. When he spoke, his voice was rough and tummy tingling.

"How about a thrill that doesn't involve anyone . . . but you and me."

He moved her hand away from her breast and lowered his water-spiked eyelashes. His gaze felt like a hot brand and her nipples hardened against the wet material of her dress.

"Damn," he whispered. "I haven't been able to stop thinking about your sweet nipples since the first night you showed them to me." His gaze lifted, his eyes reflecting the sliver of moon that had risen over the springs, turning them into two heated swirls of silver-gold. "Show them to me again, Sunshine." He released her wrist. "Please."

It was like his words were a struck match and she was a February Christmas tree. Her entire body went up in flames. There was no way she could not follow his command.

Keeping her gaze locked with his, she reached up and lowered the bodice of her dress, allowing both breasts to spring free. His breath sucked in, and she waited with trembling anticipation for him to touch her.

He didn't.

Instead, he just looked, his chest rising and falling with each uneven breath he took. It was the most sensual thing Sunny had ever experienced, standing there in the moonlight with Reid's hot gaze pinned to her. When she didn't think she could stand the anticipation a second more, he lifted his hand. His first touch was a mere brush along the side swell of her right breast.

"Jesus, you're beautiful." He wet his lips as he swept a finger over the top and around to the other side. "Do you know how many nights I've dreamed about holding these . . . worshiping them like they deserved to be worshipped?" He lightly caressed the other breast. "They just beg for attention . . . for stroking . . . for hugging." He took one in hand and gently squeezed. He growled low in his throat as his fingers tightened. "So soft . . . so damn fuckin' soft." He strummed the nipple with his thumb, causing her to moan and sway toward him. "Do you like that, baby?"

"Yes," she gasped.

"What about this?" He rolled her nipple between his calloused fingers before pinching hard. Desire zinged through her body and she had to grab on to his shoulders as her knees buckled.

He chuckled. "So my Sunshine likes it a little rough." He pinched her again before he lowered his head and took her into his hot, wet mouth with a strong suck that had her coming up to her toes and sliding her fingers through his hair.

"R-R-Reid."

He lightened the suck, his breath cooling her nipple as he spoke. "I'm right here, baby. Like I said before, I'm not going anywhere." He licked her nipple lushly before drawing it back into his mouth. While he worked his magic with his tongue and mouth, he palmed her other breast and tugged and pinched until her nipple was as hard as the pebbles beneath her feet.

But there was another part of her that badly needed attention.

Fisting his hair in her hands, she arched her back and tried to brush that needy part against his hard body. But it was impossible with him bent and worshipping her breasts. She groaned loudly in frustration and tugged on his hair.

He drew back and arched a brow. "Is there a problem, Sunshine? Is what I'm doing not thrilling enough?"

"Don't be a smart-ass. You know exactly what I need."

His eyes darkened. "And I intend to give it to you, baby. Come here." He pulled her into his arms and kissed her—a hungry kiss like he'd given her against his truck. But this time, his hands found her butt under the skirt of her dress. And since she wasn't wearing any panties, he had full access.

He growled as he tugged her against him, his fingertips brushing the crease between her butt cheeks as he palmed her in his large hands. Pressed to him, she could feel all his impressive muscles . . . including the long, hard length hidden beneath his wet trunks.

"I want to come," she said breathily as she rubbed against him.

"And I want you to come, baby. I want you to come bad." He released her butt and turned her so her back pressed against his hard chest.

"What are you—" She cut off when his lips pressed to her ear and blew softly, sending a cascade of tingles through her.

"Shh . . ." He nibbled on her lobe and those tingles tightened into a throbbing knot between her legs as he stepped back until their shoulders were submerged in the water. "Rest your head on my shoulder and just relax. I got you."

She did what he asked and her legs started to float up. His arm came around her waist and he pulled her back, anchoring her against him as his hand dipped below the skirt of her dress that floated around them.

Like with her breasts, he took his time, caressing her stomach and brushing her thighs, before he dipped between her legs and unerringly found the aching spot. As soon as his warm fingers begin their rhythmic stroke, she was lost. She couldn't think. She couldn't move. She couldn't do anything but stay in Reid's tight grip as he unraveled her.

That's how she felt. Like a sweater with a loose string of yarn that no one but Reid had ever found. With one tug, all the pretenses she had knitted together to hide her true feelings came undone. It was freeing and terrifying all at the same time. All she could do was dig her chewed-off nails into his arm and ride it out as he whispered encouragement in her ear.

"That's it, baby. Just let go."

She did. She let go. She let got and tumbled into the best orgasm of her life. When her body stopped quaking with aftershocks, he drew her close and just held her. Since she had never been one to cuddle after sex, she waited for the antsy feeling that always prompted her to pull out of a man's arms and leave. But it never showed up. As she watched the sliver of moon rise over the trees and listened to the strong beat of Reid's heart, she had no desire to be anywhere but right where she was.

He kissed her shoulder. "Thrilling enough?"

She shrugged. "Not as thrilling as pulling pranks on the townsfolk, but close."

He chuckled. "I tell you what. I'll let you paint a *t* on my butt anytime you want." He turned her around and kissed her leisurely, his hard erection pressing into her stomach. "You want to come back to my trailer?"

"I'd love to go back to your trailer."

He continued kissing her as he scooped her into his arms and walked out of the water. Unfortunately, as soon as they reached the shore, his cellphone started ringing. It turned out to be Sophie needing a ride home. Once he hung up, he looked at Sunny with disappointment in his champagne eyes.

"I'm sorry, but I have to cut our evening short."

She pinned on a smile. "No worries."

He walked over and tipped her chin up. "Oh, no. You're not going to hide behind that smile with me anymore, Sunshine. Say what you feel."

She looked into his eyes and let her smile slip. "I wish this night would never end."

"Ahh, baby." He lowered his head and kissed her with enough sexy suction to pull a moan from her. When he had her drooping against him like a piece of overcooked pasta, he drew back. "There will be other nights. I'm going to make sure of it." He gave her another quick kiss before he turned her in the direction of her car and gave her a swat on the butt. "Text me when you get home."

She drove back to the bed-and-breakfast in a daze. A month ago, she'd wanted nothing more than to climb Reid Mitchell like the Alps. But now that it looked like she was going to get to, she was having second thoughts. Not because she didn't desire him. She desired him more than she had ever desired a man in her life. If he had been any other man, she would take what she wanted and go on about her business.

But Reid wasn't just any other man.

Somewhere along the way, he'd become her friend.

A friend she had shared more with than even Cory or her Secret Sisters. She'd never cried in front of anyone, and yet, she'd sobbed her heart out with Reid. And he hadn't become upset or tried to fix it like she knew Corbin and Jesse would have. He had just held her close and let her cry. After he had given her that, how could she take what she wanted and just walk away?

And she knew that's exactly what she'd do if she started something up with Reid. She was her parents' daughter, after all. An emotional wreck who had trouble making commitments. Which was why she steered clear of them.

She needed to steer clear of Reid until she left town.

Chapter Seventeen

Reid had experienced a lot of spring-branding days in his cowboying life. But none compared to spring branding at the Holiday Ranch. When he and Sophie arrived at the branding corral that Saturday morning, he was taken back by all the trucks and trailers . . . and people. He had known the Remington men were coming to help. He had not known that their wives would be there too. Along with the other Holiday sisters and their husbands and babies. But even with all the folks scurrying around getting ready for the day, Reid's gaze had no problem zeroing in on Sunny.

He hadn't seen or talked to her since Cooper Springs. Yesterday, he'd been busy getting ready for branding. By the time he got back to the trailer, he'd had to help Sophie with a school project she'd put off until the last minute. By the time they'd finished, it had been too late to call Sunny.

But he intended to talk to her today.

And hopefully, more than talk.

Someone had set up a canopy next to a straggly

mesquite tree. Under it, Sunny was cuddling a chubby-cheeked baby in a pink bow headband. Sunny's hair was braided in a long red-tinted rope of gold that hung over one shoulder and she was looking down at the baby in her arms with a soft smile on her lips.

Reid didn't know why he felt like someone had sucker punched him in the gut. It wasn't a bad kind of pain. It was more an aching kind of longing. He had never given much thought to kids. His mind had always been too wrapped up in his dream of owning a ranch. But the sight of Sunny with the baby made him realize that he wanted kids.

He glanced over at Sophie sitting in the seat next to him.

He wanted more kids.

"Wow," Sophie said as she looked around at the chaos. "This is crazy."

Reid smiled as he parked his truck behind the others. "This is family." He jumped out to help Jace finish unloading some horses from a trailer. "Where's Hallie?"

Jace glanced at a straggly group of mesquite to their left with a concerned look. "She's not feeling so hot this morning."

Hallie came out from behind the trees looking shaky and pale. "You don't need to beat around the bush, Jace. If the way Reid has been coddling me the last few days is any indication, he knows I'm pregnant." She looked at him. "Isn't that right, Reid?"

He only shrugged. After the egg salad incident,

he'd figured things out and had been doing his darnedest to make sure Hallie didn't overdo. It wasn't an easy task. The woman was as stubborn as sin.

"I wouldn't use the word coddling. You more than pull your weight, Hallie."

She released a heavy sigh. "Yeah, well, I've come to accept that might have to change." She placed a hand on her stomach and sent Jace a determined look. "But just until this little one is out of the oven." She glanced at Reid. "Until then, I'll need to rely on my ranch manager."

He knew how hard it was for Hallie to relinquish control and he couldn't help feeling a swell of pride that she trusted him enough to relinquish it to him. "I won't let you or this ranch down, Hallie."

"I know that." She thumped his arm. "So let's get this party started."

It *did* turn out to be a party.

While the temperature was humid and hot and the work grueling, there was a festive feel to the day. Mimi and Darla had set up food on tables beneath the tarp and they and Liberty and Belle, who were both too pregnant to help with branding, passed out food and drink while the rest of the Holidays and Remingtons worked the cattle. As they separated the calves from their mamas and filed them through the chute to get tagged, branded, and vaccinated, they joked and got on each other as only family could.

Surprisingly, Reid wasn't left out of the teasing.

"Where did you learn to ride, Reid?" Casey

asked as they herded cattle into the corral. "On the mechanical horse outside your local grocery store?"

"Yep." He wheeled his horse to the left to cut off a calf from escaping. "Where did you learn to ride? On those county fair ponies that ride round and round in a circle?"

Casey laughed. "I was the best county fair pony wrangler this side of the Pecos." He whipped off his hat and waved it as his Appaloosa horse reared up on its back legs with front hoofs flailing. "Yee-haw!"

"Stop showing off, Case," Rome yelled. "I've seen you flat on your back more times than I can count."

"Same, big brother. It's just part of the joy of being a cowboy." Casey winked at Reid as he tugged on his hat. "Right, Reid?"

Reid couldn't agree more.

The sun was low in the sky by the time they finished for the day and started loading the horses back in the trailers. Reid was about to dismount and load his when he noticed Sunny sitting on her horse a few yards away. He couldn't see her face in the shadow of her straw cowboy hat, but he could feel her gaze. He didn't hesitate to walk his horse over.

"You impressed me today. I didn't realize you were a cowgirl."

She laughed. "So what impressed you most? My horrible cutting skills or my horrible roping?"

"Those take years of practice. You'll get it." If

she stayed. He wanted that. He wanted it badly. Since he hadn't heard anything about her leaving from the Holidays, he hoped the other night had changed her mind. He hoped *he* had changed her mind. "So what are you doing over here all by yourself?"

She pushed up her hat and those big brown eyes gave him the once-over. "Just enjoying the sight of hot, sweaty cowboys."

He squinted at her. "Cowboys?"

Her lips trembled with a suppressed smile. "Maybe just one."

"Hmm? So you have a thing for hot, sweaty cowboys, do ya?"

The teasing twinkle faded from her eyes. "It would seem that way. And I don't know if that's a good thing."

His stomach took a dip. "And why is that?"

She sighed and looked away. "I just don't want things to get too complicated, Reid."

He hadn't wanted that either. But now he didn't care about complications. Now all he wanted was more time with Sunny.

Uncaring that there were people around, including her two brothers, he moved his horse closer to hers and reached out and cradled her face in his hand. "I think it's too late for that." His gaze locked with hers. "I like you, Sunshine Whitlock."

She sighed. "I like you too, Reid Mitchell. But I'm not real good at commitments."

He brushed his thumb over her bottom lip, loving the way her eyes darkened. "Okay. So what about if we just take things one day at a time and see where they go? No expectations."

Her eyebrows lifted beneath the brim of her hat. "No expectations?"

He grinned. "Well, maybe a few."

"Care to elaborate?"

"How easy would it be for me to sneak into the bed-and-breakfast?"

"That depends on how quiet you are?"

He bit back a smile. "I think I can manage to be pretty quiet . . . if something worthwhile is waiting for me." He lifted her chin and leaned closer so their lips were only a breath away. "Like, say, a pretty painter with not a stitch of clothes on."

A blush stained her cheeks. "I think that can be arranged."

He really wanted to kiss her, but he figured if he did, he might lose all control and end up giving the Holidays a bigger show than he already had. So he lowered his hand and drew back.

"Then I'll see you tonight. And just so you know, I like the way you sit a saddle, Sunshine Whitlock." His gaze lowered to her jeaned thighs hugging the leather of the saddle. "I like it a lot. I like the way your curvy ass lifts and settles as you ride." He lifted his gaze to her eyes that were filled with heat. "I want you to ride me. I want you to ride me hard and long. Do you want that too, baby?"

"Yes," she said breathily. "I want that."

He smiled. "Then I guess we better get these horses loaded so you can ride tonight."

Once the horses were loaded, Mimi and Darla

insisted that everyone come over to the house for dinner to eat the rest of the food. Reid and Sophie stopped by the trailer to shower, change, and pick up Patsy Cline before they headed to the Holidays'. After the long day, Reid figured everyone would eat quickly and head home. Unfortunately, that wasn't the case. The Holidays and Remingtons didn't seem to want the party to end.

Especially after Mimi brought out her homemade elderberry wine.

It was potent stuff. So potent, it had Hank Holiday and Sam Remington, Casey and Rome's father, sitting on the porch, talking, laughing, and slapping each other's legs like they'd been friends for decades—instead of sworn enemies. Reid only had two glasses and was feeling a little unstable on his feet.

Something that didn't get past Mimi.

"I hope you're not planning on driving home, Reid. The rule is one glass of wine is fine, two and I take your keys." She held out her hand.

"No need for that, Ms. Mimi. I'm fine."

She sent him a stern look. "I'm sure you are, but now that you're a daddy, you need to set a good example. You don't want Sophie drinking and driving, do you?"

"No, ma'am, but . . ."

She held out her hand and sent him a warning look. He sighed as he reached into his pocket and handed her the keys. Damn, he couldn't catch a break. How was he going to get into town to meet Sunny without his truck?

While he was trying to figure it out, Mimi continued. "And speaking of Sophie, I've asked her to spend the night. There's a musical marathon on television and I think it's important for young people to see that true talent isn't showing how to put on makeup on that Tikity-Tok."

Reid perked up. If Sophie spent the night with the Holidays, he wouldn't have to go to town. Sunny could come to the trailer.

"Great! I'm sure Soph will love that."

Mimi smiled slyly. "And I'm sure you'll enjoy having the trailer all to yourself."

After saying his goodbyes, Reid headed home across the back pasture. On the way, he tried calling Sunny. She didn't answer so he left a text. When he got to the trailer, he wasn't sure what alerted him that he wasn't alone. Maybe it was the scent of fresh lemons that filled the air. Or maybe it was a deeper sense. Something he'd just developed.

He quickly took off his hat and slipped off his boots before heading to his bedroom.

The room was dark except for the moonlight spilling over the bed . . . and the naked woman stretched out on it.

To say Sunny took his breath away was an understatement. If he'd thought he was drunk before, it was nothing to how he felt now. He was completely intoxicated by her beauty and could only gawk like an infatuated fool.

From the tips of her peach-colored toenails to the ends of her strawberry-blond curls spilling over his pillow, she was every man's fantasy. Her breasts looked like two abundant scoops of cream topped with rose-colored nipples that bloomed into mouthwatering, hard buds beneath his gaze. Her legs were long, toned highways that led to a tiny patch of reddish-gold heaven that had him hardening beneath the fly of his jeans.

"Hey, cowboy," she said in a raspy voice that had even more desire coursing through his veins. "I heard you were interested in a ride."

"Very interested."

"Then why are you still dressed?"

"Good question." He tugged the snaps of his western shirt open and let it slip off his shoulders. When he reached for the button of his jeans, she stopped him.

"Take your time, cowboy. I want to look my fill too."

He smiled as he moved into the shaft of light coming in the window. "Whatever you want, cowgirl." He popped open the button of his jeans, then slowly rolled down his zipper. He wanted her to enjoy the show as much as he was enjoying hers, but it turned out getting jeans off wasn't easy. Or sexy. Especially when he was slightly tipsy. Once he had them to his ankles, he tried to lift his foot out and became unbalanced, nose-diving onto the bed.

As he cussed and kicked off his jeans, she giggled.

"It's not funny." He tugged off his socks and threw them across the room. "Mimi's wine is potent."

Still giggling, she rolled to her side and rested

her head in her hand. Her hair fell around her like a river of liquid moonlight, one breast peeking out of the silky strands. He didn't think he'd ever seen a prettier sight.

"Are you saying you're drunk, Reid Mitchell?" She reached out and ran her cool fingertips down the center of his chest to his belly button, leaving behind a trail of flames. "Because I wouldn't want to take advantage of an intoxicated man."

"I'm not drunk."

She sat up and pushed him back to the mattress. "I think I'll be the judge of that. Now close your eyes while I deliver a sobriety test." He closed his eyes and she leaned in closer, her warm breath falling against his face and causing a shiver of need to race through him. "Now I want you to tell me exactly what's touching you—lips or fingers." Her finger brushed over his bottom lip.

"Finger."

"Good job. And now?" She kissed him, soft and sweet.

"Lips."

"Excellent. Let's make it a little harder. Keep your eyes closed."

He didn't know if it was the anticipation, but when something brushed over his nipple, he felt it all the way down to his growing cock. He tried to stay focused, but with his erection straining against the cotton of his boxers, it was difficult.

"Finger?"

"Nope. Strike one." The touch on his nipple came again, this time with a brush of wet tongue that had him moaning. When she drew it into her hot mouth, his eyes flashed open. She released his nipple with a sucking pop he felt all the way down to his toes.

"Nuh-uh. No peeking or I'm going to think you are too inebriated to ride tonight."

He slammed his eyes closed and waited for her next touch. He felt a light touch on his stomach. A finger, definitely a finger, dipped into his belly button before tracing the line of hair to the waistband of his boxers where it brushed back and forth with tingling heat.

He swallowed hard. "Finger."

"Good boy," she whispered next to his ear.

The mattress shifted and he felt the brush of soft skin on either side of his thighs. He barely had time to register that she was straddling him when his boxers were tugged down and his rock-hard cock set free.

He heard her swift intake of breath and then nothing but silence.

Lying there so exposed with his eyes closed made him feel vulnerable and, at the same time, excited as hell. When something brushed over the tip of his cock, he felt like he'd been stunned with an electric cattle prod.

"Lips or fingers?" she asked.

He struggled to think, let alone speak. "L-L-Lips."

"Nope. Strike two."

Damn. He focused his entire attention on her next touch. He wasn't about to strike out. But when it came, he lost all thought as he was engulfed in the wet heat of her mouth.

"Sunshine," he growl-groaned as his fingers tangled in her hair and his hips rose off the mattress. "Sweet Sunshine."

Chapter Eighteen

Sunny had never much cared for her first name. It was too cheerful. Too bright. Too pure. But when Reid said it in his husky, desire-filled voice, it didn't sound cheerful, bright, and pure.

It sounded sensual. Dark. Dirty.

She liked it. She liked it a lot.

Before Reid, pleasing men she spent the night with hadn't been high on her list. She'd been more concerned with them pleasing her. But she wanted to please Reid. And she didn't just want to please him. She wanted to drive him wild with desire.

She seemed to be doing a good job of it. His eyes were squeezed closed as if he were in pain as he fisted his hands in the sheets and moaned. The tensing of his thighs and abdominal muscles told her he was close. But before she could bring him to release, he spoke in a choked voice.

"St-op!"

She lifted her head and looked at him with concern. "Did I hurt you?"

He cradled her face in his hand and shook his head. "God, no. I just want you right there with me when I come."

It was about the sweetest thing she'd ever heard. She moved up his hard body, intending to give him a soft kiss of gratitude, but he quickly took control of her lips in a possessive kiss that wiped all thoughts from her mind save for one.

More.

She wanted more.

He gave it to her.

As he kissed her, his hands slowly wandered over her body as if he was memorizing every curve and dip. When those work-roughened fingers finally slipped between her legs, parting her folds and dipping into her wet heat, his moan was as loud as hers.

"You are so hot, baby," he whispered against her lips. "So damn hot. Can I have this?" He dipped deeper and strummed her with his thumb. Liquid desire spread through her and she would have given him just about anything.

"P-P-Please, Reid."

He growled low and gave her one more body-melting finger-thrust and thumb-strum before he pulled away and reached for the drawer of his nightstand. When he returned with a condom, she couldn't help teasing him.

"Just how long have those been in your drawer, Reid Mitchell?"

He grinned, sheepishly. "Since I met you. I think my subconscious knew where this was headed long before I did. Or maybe it was just wishful thinking." His smile faded as his eyes darkened. "So are you gonna grant my wish, Sunshine?"

She took the condom from him. "I'm gonna grant both our wishes."

She took her time putting on the condom, enjoying the feel of his hard length in her hand. If his moans were any indications, he seemed to be enjoying it too. They both were breathing hard by the time she straddled him.

She hadn't ever given much thought to how she and men fit. Probably because she'd never fit with a man like she fit with Reid. Once she was fully seated, they both groaned with satisfaction. That feeling of satisfaction only grew as she started to move up and down his thick shaft.

At first, he allowed her to set the pace, but then his hands gripped her hips and he took control, meeting each one of her pumps with a hard thrust that turned desire into gnawing, frenzied need.

"Harder," she moaned as she flung her head back and clawed at his chest. "I want it harder."

She released a squeak of surprise when he flipped her to her back. Pinning her hands to the mattress with one hand and holding the majority of his weight with the other, he gave her what she asked for.

She felt like she was incinerating from the inside out. The tighter his grip on her wrists and the harder he thrust, the more she burned.

"You like it rough, don't you, baby?" he gritted out between his teeth as he thrust into her deep. "You like it when you aren't treated like a fragile doll. Well, I'll never treat you like a fragile doll, Sunshine. Because you're a strong woman who can take what she wants. So take it, baby." He pumped faster. "Take it."

The mixture of his dirty talk and hard thrusts sent her flying right over the edge and into the spiraling vortex of an earth-shattering orgasm that seemed to go on forever. Somewhere in the midst of it, she felt him find his own release with a tightening of muscles and a loud curse.

When it was over and Reid had released her wrists and slumped on top of her, she felt like one of Darla's dishrags that had been wrung out and left to dry on the oven handle.

A content dishrag.

With other men, the moments after sex had always been filled with a multitude of emotions—disappointment, awkwardness, the need to make sure the guy didn't become too clingy. Which probably explained why she'd always made a quick exit or asked them to leave. But lying there with Reid draped over her, she didn't feel awkward or dissatisfied. And she certainly wasn't in any hurry to leave. In fact, she felt like she could stay right there in the haven of Reid's big, muscled body forever.

"You need to let me go, Sunny."

Her face flamed as she realized she was holding on to him like a barnacle to the hull of a ship. "Oh! Sorry."

As soon as she released him, he pushed up to his hands and looked down at her. "There's no reason to apologize. I like being held in your arms. I like it a lot. If I hadn't been worried about crushing you, I could have fallen asleep right there."

She felt her heart warm. "I like being in your arms too."

He smiled a satisfied smile. "Good. If you give me a second, I'll have you back there." He dipped down and delivered a kiss that had her body humming all over again before he got out of bed. He returned only moments later and delivered on his promise, pulling her into his arms and holding her like he never wanted to let her go.

After the long day of work and great sex, she should be tired. But she didn't feel tired. She felt wide awake . . . and content.

"Tell me about your childhood," she said as she played with his chest hair. "Where did you grow up?"

"Waco."

"With your mama, daddy, and sister?"

He stopped drawing circles on her bare shoulder with his thumb. "Just my mama and sister. Our daddy was mostly out of the picture." She felt his muscles tense. "He wasn't married to my mom. He had a wife and family that he spent most of his time with."

Her heart tightened. "I'm sorry."

"It was okay. I had my mama and my sister."

She hesitated. "What happened to your sister?"

There was a long pause before he spoke. "Pancreatic cancer. She only lived five months after her diagnosis."

"I'm so sorry, Reid."

"Me too. Even though we weren't nearly as

close as you and Corbin, I loved her. I didn't realize how much until she was gone." He paused. "I wish I'd been a better brother. I wish I had told her how much I loved her."

Sunny lifted her head and looked at him. "I think she knew. You proved it by showing up when she needed you the most."

He sighed. "But I wasn't happy about it. Poor Sophie. The kid lost her mom and then got stuck with an inept cowboy who doesn't know the first thing about being a parent."

"Maybe you didn't know the first thing about it then, but you're a fast learner. Sophie couldn't ask for a better guardian."

He sent her a skeptical look. "Now you're just lying to make me feel better."

"Not at all. Believe me, I know a good guardian when I see one. I had my fair share of bad ones."

His gaze turned sad. "Corbin mentioned how tough your childhood was." He brushed a strand of hair behind her ear. "I'm sorry you had to go through that, Sunshine."

"Like you, it was okay because I had someone who loved me. I owe Corbin so much."

"Is that why you keep all your anger and unhappiness hidden from him? Why you try to be his perfect little sister?"

His blunt words had her sitting up. "I'm not perfect. I'm far from it."

Reid studied her, his gaze direct. "You're right. You aren't perfect, Sunny. No one is. People get mad and grumpy and have bad days. No one can be sunny all the time. Sometimes the rain clouds move in and you just feel like . . . turning a *but* into a *butt*." He reached out and took her hand in his. "And that's okay. It's okay to show your angry art, Sunny."

Talk about rain clouds. She couldn't keep her eyes from filling with tears and rolling down to her cheeks. When she went to wipe them away and make some silly excuse for her sudden emotional state, Reid stopped her.

"Let them fall, Sunshine. To me, your tears are just as beautiful as your smiles—your angry art just as stunning as your landscapes." He drew her back into his arms and kissed the top of her head. "Now all you have to do is realize that too."

Sunny woke with the strong need to create. It had been such a long time since she'd felt that need she couldn't ignore it. Carefully easing out from beneath Reid's arm, she got up and grabbed his western shirt and pulled it on before she went hunting for a sketchpad and pencil.

When she'd lived in the trailer, she'd tucked her art supplies in every nook and cranny in case inspiration hit. So it didn't take her long to find a sketchpad and pencils in the cabinet of an end table. Once she had them in hand, she grabbed a kitchen chair and hurried back to Reid's room. He was still sound asleep and she wasted no time getting to work.

Worried the creative energy would disappear at any second, she worked feverishly, her pencil flying over the paper like it had a will of its own.

Seconds later, Reid's image took shape. Sleep-mussed hair falling like a ruffled raven's wing over a high forehead. Thick eyelashes resting just above sleep-flushed cheekbones. Dark scruff covering an uneven top lip and angular jaw.

After sketching his face, she moved to his perfectly-sculptured shoulders and chest. She was so focused on getting the muscles around his collarbone just right that she didn't realize Reid was awake until he shifted. She glanced to his face to find his pretty amber eyes on her.

She pointed the pencil at him. "Don't you dare move another muscle."

A smile tipped his mouth. "Or what?"

She thought for only a moment. "I'll leave."

The smile disappeared. "Can I keep my eyes open? I like watching you draw. Especially in my shirt." His gaze lowered. "And the view would be even better if you opened your legs just a little bit."

She bit back a smile. "Pervert. Now don't move." She went back to sketching . . . with her legs slightly wider than before. Reid kept his word and remained perfectly still until she was almost finished.

"I hate to mess with your creativity, sweetheart, but I need to go to the bathroom in a bad way."

"Okay. Just let me—"

"No time." He threw back the sheet, jumped out of bed, and hurried out of the room. When offered such a delightful display of hard male virility, Sunny didn't complain. Besides, the drawing was close to being done. And pretty good if she did say so herself. Still, she didn't feel confident enough to share her work and quickly closed the sketchpad as soon as Reid stepped back into the room.

He lifted his eyebrows. "So I guess I don't get to see it."

"Nope." She tucked the sketchpad and pencil under the chair.

He shrugged. "Okay. I guess I'll have to live with you being shy about your work." His gaze ran over her. "What I can't live with is that shirt."

She glanced down. "What's wrong with it?"

"It's still on you."

She glanced up to see him smiling evilly. Smiling evilly with an impressive erection. Desire swelled up like sweet honey from a cracked-open hive. She rose to her feet, and slowly unsnapped the shirt and let it slip from her shoulders. Before it even hit the ground, Reid had her on the bed, her hands over her head and his hard, muscled body pressing into her.

He moved his lips along her throat, punctuating each word he spoke with a nibbling kiss. "I—was—doing—a—little—thinking—while—you—were—sketching."

She pressed her hips against his erection. "I gathered that."

He lifted his head and grinned. "Noticed that, did ya?"

"It's hard not to notice. Pardon the pun."

He laughed. She could get drunk on his laughter. It made her as giddy as Mimi's elderberry wine.

She smoothed his hair off his forehead. "So what were you thinking about exactly, Reid Mitchell?"

"I was thinking about how fun it would be if you painted me."

"You want me to paint you?"

"Not like a portrait. I want you to use my body like a canvas . . . for your angry art."

Reid had done a lot of dirty talking in the last twelve hours, but this . . . this not only set her body aflame, it also caused a flame to flicker to life in her heart. For the first time in her life, she felt seen. Really seen. While she knew what to do about the fire burning low in her body, she didn't have a clue what to do with the fire burning deep in her heart.

Reid misunderstood her hesitation. "What? Too kinky?"

"No . . . I just . . . would like that." She smiled. "I'd like that a lot."

"Then it's a date." He kissed her sweetly. "Tonight, I'm going to stretch out on that art table of yours and let you do your worst." His eyes darkened. "But for now, I want to do a little painting of my own." He bent his head and brushed his tongue along her neck in a heated trail of fire. "I think I'm going to call this . . . Sunshine art."

It turned out he was extremely good at Sunshine art. Using his tongue and lips, he painted her body into a trembling canvas of need. When he reached the tattoo on her hip, he lightly kissed each petal as if adding the most delicate highlights before moving down a few inches to her quivering center. With all his prep work, all it took was one deep kiss and a few flicks of his tongue to send her flying.

He stayed with her until the last tremor and sigh. Then he lifted his head and smiled smugly.

"Not to shabby for my first work of art."

Before she could answer, the front door opened.

"Uncle Reid! I'm home!"

Reid and Sunny stared at each other in horror for only a second before springing from the bed like a couple of naughty teenagers caught by their parents. Reid grabbed his jeans while Sunny grabbed his shirt.

But before they could even start to get dressed, Sophie appeared in the doorway. They both tried to hide like shy virgins behind the piece of clothing they held as Sophie looked between them in disbelief.

Reid finally broke the awkward silence with an angry bellow. "Get out, Sophie!"

She flinched before she turned and hurried down the hallway, followed by the slamming of the front door.

"Shit!" Reid tugged on his jeans before racing after her.

Sunny hadn't even finished getting dressed when he returned looking like a wild man.

"She took your car!"

Chapter Nineteen

"Sophie's being taken to the county hospital."

Reid clutched his cellphone and tried to comprehend the words Sheriff Decker Carson had just spoken, but his brain couldn't. He removed his arm from around Sunny and got up from the couch. "What do you mean she's been taken to the hospital?"

Sunny jumped up and stared at him. "Sophie's hurt?"

He didn't answer her. He was too focused on Decker's reply.

"The ambulance is leaving the crash site now."

Crash site? Reid felt like his heart dropped to his feet as fear knifed through him. "Is she okay?"

"She's conscious, but pretty banged up." Decker hesitated. "She was asking for you."

"I'm on my way." He hung up and headed straight for the door, thankful that earlier he and Sunny had made the trek to the Holidays and gotten his truck. Sunny hurried after him.

"What happened?"

Exactly what he'd been worried was going to happen. But he'd let Sunny talk him out of calling the police or going after her. He'd let her convince him that Sophie had just taken a little harmless joyride and would be back anytime. But it looked like Sophie hadn't just gone on a harmless joyride. She'd gotten in an accident on the highway.

A serious accident.

He ignored Sunny's question and got in his truck. He wasn't in the mood for company, but she hopped into the passenger seat before he could stop her. Which wasn't a good thing. When they passed the site of the accident and he saw Sunny's totaled car being hooked to a tow truck, his composure snapped and fear had him lashing out in anger.

"Why would you leave your keys in your car? What the hell were you thinking?"

Sunny looked over at him in stunned shock. "I'm sorry. I didn't think anyone would steal my car on the Holiday Ranch."

"Why would you think that when you witnessed firsthand Sophie stealing my truck?"

"Sophie wasn't there. If she had been, I wouldn't have been there."

He looked back at the road. "Maybe you shouldn't have been."

He knew it was a hurtful thing to say, but it was the truth. Sunny shouldn't have been there. If she hadn't been, Sophie wouldn't be in the hospital right now. Of course, it wasn't Sunny's fault as much as his. He had worked so hard to get where he'd gotten with Sophie and he'd thrown it all away because he couldn't keep his pants up.

And now Sophie was the one who would pay.

He fisted the steering wheel and tried to get a grip on his fear. "Look, I'm sorry. I shouldn't be blaming you. Not when it's my fault. I was the one who started this. But you need to know that I can't be the type of person who shirks his responsibilities just for a cheap thrill."

"A cheap thrill?"

He glanced over at her. "Come on, Sunny. That's all I was to you and you know it. You've made it perfectly clear you aren't the type of woman who likes commitments. Are you saying that has changed?"

She stared at him for only a moment before she looked away, her lips pressed in a firm line. "You're right. A cheap thrill was all it was."

He didn't know why her words hurt so much—especially when he had handed them to her on a silver platter. Maybe because he'd hoped she'd deny them and say she was staying. He should have known better. Sunny was a free spirit. No man would ever be able to hold her in one place. Not even her beloved brother could.

She had warned him about not being able to commit. And yet, he still couldn't stay away from her. He now understood how his sister and mama had fallen for men who couldn't commit. Sunny had his father's carefree attitude about life. Maybe that was what had attracted him all along.

He'd been looking for his father's love.

The pain of that epiphany mixed with his fear

for Sophie had him spending the rest of the drive to the hospital in silent misery. Once there, a woman at the front desk of the emergency wing directed him to a room.

Reid didn't realize Sunny wasn't following him until he reached the room and glanced back to see her standing by the front desk, looking heartbreakingly sad. He knew her sadness had more to do with Sophie than the end of whatever they'd had together. He looked at her for one brief moment longer before he pulled his gaze away and walked into the room.

If he had thought he felt guilty before, it was nothing compared to what he felt when he saw Sophie lying in bed looking bruised and battered. Her face had multiple cuts and she wore a neck brace.

Emotion swelled in his chest.

He didn't know how it had happened, but he loved this ornery teen. He loved her as much as he'd loved her mama.

"Hey, Soph."

She jerked her gaze from the nurse who was adjusting her IV. Her eyes, eyes just like his, welled with tears. He didn't hesitate to walk over and carefully pull her into his arms.

She melted against him and started to sob. "I'm—so—sorry, Uncle—Reid."

He kissed the top of her head. "No, I'm sorry. I screwed up. But I'm not going to screw up again. I promise, Soph. I won't screw up again."

Thankfully, Sophie's x-rays came back showing no broken bones or internal injuries. The cuts on her face from the flying glass didn't even need stitches and when the doctor removed the neck collar, Sophie had no problems moving her head.

She was lucky, especially after hearing the details of the accident. She had been trying to pass a truck pulling a trailer hauling hay. When she'd seen a car coming in the opposite lane, she'd pulled back too quickly and clipped the bumper of the hay trailer. She'd spun out of control and hit a utility pole, causing the car to barrel-roll.

It was a miracle she had survived with only a few scratches and bruises.

Once she got her clean bill of health from the doctor and was released, Reid's concern turned more to anger. He planned to give her a piece of his mind as soon as they were in his truck. But his plans had to wait. When they stepped into the lobby, he discovered it overflowing with Holidays and Remingtons.

Mimi, Darla, and the Holiday sisters clustered around Sophie, giving her hugs and words of sympathy, while the men showed their concern with gentle pats on Sophie's back and hearty thumps on Reid's. He could tell Sophie felt as overwhelmed as he did. She started to cry while he graciously thanked everyone for coming.

Or not everyone.

There was someone obviously missing.

He couldn't help the disappointment that settled in his stomach as he looked around for Sunny. Of course, he couldn't blame her for not being there. Especially after the way he'd talked to her. He had let his fear turn him into some kind of raving lunatic. He wanted to call her and take back all the things he'd said to her, but then realized it was probably for the best if he just left things the way they were. Even if she wasn't leaving now, she would leave eventually. Starting something up with her was just a dead end road.

On the way home, he started to give Sophie a stern lecture, but when he glanced over at her, he couldn't do it. Not when she looked like she'd been through hell. He figured postponing the conversation for another day wouldn't be bad parenting. So once they got back to the trailer, he made her favorite frozen pizza and they ate it on the couch as they watched Patsy Cline do her obstacle course around the trailer.

After they finished eating, he collected their plates and took them to the kitchen. "You should probably go to bed, Soph. It's been a long day and you need to get some rest." He knew he needed sleep. He felt completely drained—both physically and emotionally.

She brought her glass to the sink. "Do I have to go to school tomorrow? Everyone will be talking about what happened and how stupid I am."

It looked like they were going to have this conversation after all.

He shut off the water and dried his hands before he leaned back against the counter and crossed his arms. "What you did was stupid. And reckless and immature and irresponsible. You endangered, not only your life, but others'. You're lucky no one was seriously injured . . . or dead. And when you finally prove to me that you're mature and responsible enough to get your license and drive—which isn't going to be anytime soon—you'll have to get a job and pay for your own insurance. With this accident on your records, it won't be cheap."

She looked down at the floor and nodded solemnly. "I know. You probably hate me for embarrassing you in front of the entire town."

He lifted her chin and looked in her teary eyes. "I don't hate you, Soph. I love you." He'd failed to tell his sister how much he loved her before she passed. He wasn't going to make the same mistake with Sophie. And he wasn't just going to tell her. He was going to show her.

He pulled her into his arms and hugged her close.

Tears soaked into his T-shirt. "I love you too, Uncle Reid. I'm sorry for how I acted. Not just the accident, but for running away like a little kid when I saw you and Sunny."

He really didn't want to have this discussion, but he knew he had to. "I'm sorry you saw . . . what you saw. I don't want you thinking that it's okay to sleep around with people. Because it's not. You should wait to share that with someone you really care about."

She drew back, her eyes confused. "So you don't care about Sunny?"

He'd stepped into that one. "I do care about Sunny. But last night was just . . ." Anything but a cheap thrill. At least for him. It had been the most amazing night of his life. He cleared his throat. "It just happened."

"So you aren't going to marry her?"

"Marry her? Why would you think that?"

"Because it's obvious you really like her. You were so sad before and then Sunny showed up and you weren't sad anymore. She makes you happy. And I wasn't upset y'all were having sex." She swallowed hard before she continued. "I was upset because I thought if y'all got married, there wouldn't be any room in your life for me."

Reid stared at her. "Why would you ever think that, Soph? You're my family. There will always be room in my life for you."

She stared at him. "Mama was your family too and you cut her out of your life."

He heaved a sigh. "You're right. I did. And I was wrong. Your mama was . . ." He searched for the right word. Sophie found it first.

"Chaotic?"

He smiled. "Yes. And I have never much cared for chaos. I wanted my life to be nice and neat and calm. I thought if I bought a ranch and lived out in the middle of nowhere with nothing for company but cattle and horses, I could avoid all the drama that comes with people and relationships. But then your mama called. And yes, it was painful to watch her die, but I wouldn't trade those last few months we had together for all the ranches in Texas." He reached out and tweaked her nose. "Nor would I trade you."

"Even though I'm chaotic too?"

"You're a teenager who just lost her mama and is stuck with a clueless uncle who doesn't know the first thing about being a good parent. I think it's understandable that you feel a little chaotic."

She grinned. "You might have been clueless to begin with, but I think you're doing an okay job now."

He laughed. "Thanks. Now you need to go get ready for bed—just in case you change your mind and want to go to school."

She started to turn, but then stopped. "It's okay if you have sex with Sunny, Uncle Reid."

His face heated. "Well . . . I don't think we need to talk about that."

She rolled her eyes. "I'm not a kid. I can talk about sex. And you don't need to worry about me running out and having sex with some boy just because you and Sunny do. I've figured out I'm not ready for that. But you're old and old people should have healthy sexual relationships. It would be weird if you didn't." She hesitated. "If you ever wanted to marry Sunny, that would be okay with me too. I like her."

Reid didn't know why that made him feel like crying.

"I don't think me and Sunny are going to work out. She's not the marrying type. But maybe this *old man* can find someone else to date so his niece doesn't think he's weird."

"They won't be as much fun as Sunny."

No, they wouldn't be. No one was as much fun as Sunny. She was a light.

A light that couldn't be held.

Once Sophie went to bed, Reid took a long,

hot shower and then headed to his own room. He hadn't been in it since that morning and seeing the sex-rumpled sheets was a sucker punch. All the images of the night before flooded back and he didn't know how long he stood there staring at the bed before he shook himself and headed to the dresser to get a pair of boxers. On the way, he noticed the kitchen chair . . . and the sketchpad beneath.

Part of him wanted to take a peek inside and the other part wanted to burn it. Maybe he'd do both. Take a peek and then burn it. But when he opened it and saw the sketch Sunny had drawn of him, he was the one who felt burned. It wasn't the obvious talent of the artist that took his breath away. It was the subject that left him feeling blindsided.

Reid almost didn't recognize the man staring back at him. This man wasn't a lone cowboy who avoided people and chaos. The man sketched on the paper looked like a man who lived life to the fullest. You could see it in the mischievous twinkle in his eyes and the slight tilt of his lips that he wasn't the type of man who planned everything and worried about what tomorrow would bring. He was a relaxed, carefree man who lived for the moment.

The type of man who easily laughed . . . and easily loved.

Love shone from his eyes like a beacon.

Seeing that love so blatantly illustrated completely broadsided Reid. This was how Sunny viewed him? This was the man she saw when she looked at him? Or maybe this was the man he became when she was with him.

A better man.

He was still trying to process everything when his cellphone rang. He didn't realize how much he wanted it to be Sunny until his heart dropped with disappointment when he saw Corbin's name on the screen. He thought about not answering it. But then realized he had to. Corbin was his boss.

"Hey, Mr. Whitlock. Is there a problem at the ranch?"

"No. There's another problem I'd like to discuss. Can you come over to my house?"

"Sure. I'll be right there."

It didn't take him long to get dressed and drive to Corbin and Belle's house. Corbin was waiting for him on the front porch. Which made Reid feel more than a little uneasy.

As soon as he stepped onto the porch, Corbin nodded at a chair. "Have a seat."

Reid sat down. "If this is about Sophie wrecking Sunny's car, I have already turned it over to my insurance and they said they'd take care of everything."

"It's not about Sunny's car, Reid." Corbin hesitated. "It's about her heart."

All Reid could do was stare at him. "Her heart?"

Corbin studied him. "I'd like to know why, today at the hospital, Sunny was so upset."

"I'm sure she was just concerned about Sophie."

"I thought the same until we found out Sophie was just fine and Sunny still looked like she had every time our parents dumped us off on another relative." He stared Reid down. "Like someone she loves didn't love her enough to want to keep her. I figured that someone was you when she raced off to the bathroom as soon as you and Sophie stepped into the lobby."

Just the thought of Sunny loving him made his stomach feel like he'd just been tossed from a horse and was freefalling. Of course, it wasn't true. It couldn't be. "She doesn't love me."

"Are you sure about that? People think Sunny is just a frivolous carefree young woman who does things on a whim. But that's not true. Before she makes any decision, she considers all the repercussions. Mostly because she doesn't want her actions to hurt anyone. I'm sure she thought about painting the *t* on the Nothin' But Muffins sign for weeks before she actually did it. She wouldn't randomly fall in bed with a man—especially the foreman of my ranch and a young girl's guardian—unless she had strong feelings."

"But she's leaving."

Corbin smiled sadly. "Of course, she is. That's how she protects her heart. She leaves before someone can leave her."

It was like a huge light bulb went on in Reid's head. He had thought the sketch Sunny had drawn that morning was of a man who could love. That was true. But Sunny wouldn't have seen that love unless she'd been looking for it. Unless she loved him as much as he loved her.

"Holy shit," he whispered. "Sunny loves me."

Corbin sighed. "I think that's what I've been trying to tell you."

Reid didn't know what to do with the revelation. He felt stunned and overwhelmed . . . and completely unworthy. "But how could she love me? I mean she could get anyone she wants."

Corbin sent him a pointed look. "I think all Sunny wants is to be loved by someone who won't ever let her go."

Reid had done just the opposite. He was so upset about Sophie that he'd pushed Sunny away. When things got tough, he'd abandoned her without a backward glance. Just like he had done to his sister. Obviously, Sunny wasn't the only one who pushed people away because they were scared of getting hurt.

"Shit." He rested his elbows on his knees and covered his face with his hands. "I'm such an idiot. I was so busy guarding my own heart that I didn't realize I was breaking hers."

"So you love her?"

He lowered his hands and looked at Corbin. "Yes. I love her. But I think it might be too late to prove it after how I treated her."

"I thought the same thing with my wife, but I found out that it's never too late to prove you love someone. Although, after all Sunny's been through, it might take declaring your love on a New York Times Square billboard to get her to believe you."

A Times Square billboard?

Reid smiled. "I think I might know of something that would work even better."

All he needed was paint . . . and the nerve to take a step on the wild side.

Chapter Twenty

Most women might be heartbroken that the man they had started to have feelings for had rejected them like a holey, mismatched sock. But most women hadn't been raised like Sunny. They hadn't been rejected over and over again until their heart had formed a thick outer shell that nothing could penetrate.

Okay, so maybe her heart did feel a little battered. But it wasn't anything she couldn't deal with. She was a strong woman who was in control of her emotions.

Although hiding out in the emergency room bathroom as soon as Reid and Sophie stepped into the lobby wasn't exactly the action of a strong woman. But she didn't want to put Reid, or herself, in an awkward situation. So she'd hidden out until they'd left, then caught a ride home with Corbin, Belle, Jesse, and Liberty.

Corbin seemed to know something wasn't right and kept shooting her glances in the rearview mirror the entire drive back to the bed-and-breakfast. She knew he was going to want to interrogate her. So as soon as they got there, she used the excuse of being tired and went to her room.

She *was* tired, but she didn't go to bed.

Instead, she grabbed a blank canvas, while Jimmy hurled obscenities at her, and started to paint. The painting didn't turn out angry as much as miserably sad. Ultramarine blue was the predominant color, and rather than throw it, she dripped it down the gray base-coated canvas like the tears that dripped down her cheeks.

She didn't try to push back those tears. She was through hiding her emotions. Through putting on a bright smile and acting like everything was just fine and dandy so she wouldn't be pitied or upset the people she loved. Like everyone else in the world, she had the right to be angry. To cry. To throw fits. To paint angry art. She was who she was and people could love her or not.

That included Reid Mitchell.

It also included her mama and daddy.

After she finished the painting, she cleaned her brushes, gave Jimmy more birdseed to throw on the floor, and then called her parents. Her mama answered with her usual enthusiasm.

Her mama was good at hiding her true emotions too.

"Hey, my sweet little ray of sunshine! It's about time you called your mama. Didn't you get all my messages?" Sunny had gotten them. She had just been putting off dealing with them. But she couldn't put it off anymore.

"I got them."

There was a long pause. "Well, if you got them, I didn't receive the money. Did you Venmo me?"

"No, Mama, I didn't."

"Oh. So are you gonna send a check this time?"

"No. No check. I'm not sending you any more money, Mama."

"What? Why? If this is about me not answering your call last month, your daddy and I had just gotten into an argument and I wasn't fit company. You know how I get when me and your daddy fight. I just want to be alone."

A great sadness filled her. Her mama would never change. Sunny had to accept that.

"Yes, I know how you get, Mama. In fact, if anyone knows how you get, it's me and Corbin. We were the pawns in your and Daddy's pathetic marriage. We were the ones who suffered the most every time you fought. And I'm through pretending that we didn't." Emotion rose in her throat and it was a struggle to get the next words out. "I'm also through trying to make you love me. If you can't love me, that's your loss. Not mine."

Before her mama could reply, she hung up the phone. Her heart hurt and her hands shook, but she also felt like a huge weight had been lifted from her shoulders. She felt lighter than she'd felt in a long time. Maybe forever.

She also felt drained.

Stripping out of her paint clothes, she crawled into bed and fell fast asleep.

She woke in the morning to a loud "Bullshit!"

She rolled to her back to find Jimmy Buffett perched on her painting. She sent him an annoyed look. "What's bullshit to some folks is art to others."

As soon as the words were out of her mouth, she remembered a study one of her favorite art instructors had talked about where a group of people from different walks of life had been shown ten paintings from famous artists and asked to rate them from their favorite to least favorite. Out of fifty random people, no two had rated the paintings exactly the same. In fact, the ratings were widely spread with some people rating a certain painting high and others rating the same painting low.

The study had proven that art was in the eye of the beholder.

And yet, Sunny had been letting a few art critics and a couple bad showings convince her that she had no talent.

For the first time, she really studied her angry art. She realized that she didn't hate it. She liked it. She liked it a lot. It *was* a piece of her. A sad piece, but still a piece. She was tired of being ashamed of her pieces. She was tired of hiding her art.

With a burst of energy that startled Jimmy and sent him flying to the top of his cage, she jumped out of bed and pulled on her paint-splattered T-shirt and jeans before grabbing the painting from the easel.

The door of the gallery wasn't locked. There was no art inside to steal. But there was going to be.

It was time Sunny came out of the attic.

There was an entire gallery full of empty walls to hang the painting, but she chose to set "Wall of Tears" on the easel in the front window. Once the painting was secure, she walked outside to take a look.

It looked good.

It looked damn good.

A joyful bark had her turning from the gallery window. Buck came waddling out the back door of the house to greet her, stopping to lift his leg on a bush on the way. Jesse wasn't far behind him, wearing a stretched-out T-shirt, saggy sweatpants, and a sleepy look.

He yawned widely as he stood next to her and looked at the painting. "Is that new?"

"Yes. What do you think?"

"Hmm?" He shut one eye and squinted the other. "I think it's not as good as the Holidays' barn picture you painted for me and Liberty for our wedding, but much better than that famous painting by that artist who chopped off his own ear. But that's the funny thing about art. Everyone likes something different."

She smiled as she looked at the painting. "I'm just starting to figure that out."

"So you've become an abstract impressionist?"

She realized she didn't know the answer to that question. She also realized that it didn't matter. "I don't know. I think I'm just going to paint what I want to—whether it's abstract or a big red barn."

Jesse looked at her. "Does this mean you're not moving to Dallas to do web design?"

She looked at the gallery Corbin had lovingly

gifted her, then into Jesse's brown eyes that were so much like hers. "I think it does."

He let out a whoop and swung her up in his arms. She was still laughing when he set her back on her feet and gave her a serious look. "Does this have anything to do with Reid Mitchell?"

Just hearing his name made her heart feel like it had been stomped on by a herd of cattle. Normally, she would swallow the pain and pin a smile on her face. But her days of smiling when she didn't feel like it were over. "No. Whatever I had with Reid is over."

His eyes turned sad. "I guess that's why you looked so wrung out yesterday."

"I'm still feeling pretty wrung out. But I think I'll be okay."

"Of course you'll be okay. You have my and Corbin's blood running through your veins. Us Cates-Whitlocks are resilient as cockroaches." He put her in a headlock and rubbed her head with his knuckles until she giggled. "Now let's go get some muffins. If Liberty wakes up and doesn't have something to fill her mama belly, she's one grouchy woman."

She playfully shoved him away. "Just let me run in and get some shoes and my phone."

She easily found her flip-flops, but she couldn't seem to find her phone. Since the last time she'd had it, she'd been sitting on the bed talking to her mama, she searched through the mussed covers before getting down on her hands and knees to see if she'd knocked it off last night.

She found it under the bed . . . along with

another one of Mrs. Fields's letters. It must have slipped off the bed the day she and Liberty had been reading them. When she saw the paper clip, she realized it was the letter that had been clipped to the one she'd given Corbin. Even though Jesse was waiting, she couldn't help opening the envelope.

This letter was handwritten, not typed, and not nearly as threatening.

Dear Mrs. Fields,

I have arrived safely and, besides a little nausea, the trip was uneventful. The hotel is not as nice as the boardinghouse, but it's more than adequate ... with no customers to worry about pleasing. I can't thank you enough for making all the arrangements and getting me a bus ticket. You have always been kind to me and I wanted to make sure you know I would never do anything to cause trouble for you. This is my child. No one else's. I have no desire to see Wilder or Ulysses again. Although I do miss you and the girls. Give everyone my love.

Sincerely,

Ima Lee Rhimes

Sunny stared at the letter in her hand. A baby? The hush money was about Mrs. Stokes's daddy impregnating one of the women who had worked for Mrs. Fields? If that was true, then Mrs. Stokes could have a half sibling somewhere.

She picked up her phone to call Corbin, but before she could, it started ringing. She knew it wasn't Reid. He'd made it clear whatever they had was over. But she couldn't stop herself from hoping. She quickly answered.

"Hello?"

"Hi, Sunny." Sophie's tentative voice came through the receiver. "It's me . . . Sophie Mitchell." She hurried on. "I know you're probably not real happy to hear from me. Especially after what I did to your car and the way I acted yesterday and all . . . and I'm sorry." Her voice cracked. "I'm real sorry."

Sunny knew she shouldn't be a softie. But she was. Especially where Sophie was concerned.

"Oh, honey, it's okay—I mean, not okay. You shouldn't have run off like you did. And you really shouldn't have stolen my car. You could have been seriously hurt. Or worse, you could have . . . I don't even want to think about what could have happened. I just want you to promise me you'll never do anything like that again."

"I swear I won't! I had a long talk with Uncle Reid and I don't feel so icky anymore." Sophie hesitated. "I think he kinda likes me."

"Of course he does, Sophie. He loves you."

"Yeah, and I don't have a clue why when I'm such a pain in the butt."

"You had a pretty good reason to be. But take it from someone who knows, acting out doesn't help the icky feelings as much as pushes them down deeper. Eventually, you'll still have to deal with what's making you feel icky."

Sophie heaved a sigh. "I know." Again, there was a hesitation. "Hopefully, you'll be around to help me with that."

Sunny started to say that them being friends might not be a good idea, but then stopped. Just because Reid had made it clear he didn't want to have a relationship with Sunny that didn't mean Sunny couldn't have a relationship with Sophie.

"I will be," she said firmly. "And I'll help you any way I can."

"Yay! Now I can get to the real reason I called."

"The real reason?"

"Uncle Reid is in jail. Since it's your fault, I figured you should be the one to bail him out."

Chapter Twenty-one

SUNNY WAS STILL in a state of shock when Jesse drove her to the sheriff's office.

"It doesn't make any sense," she said. "Reid is the last person that would do anything criminal."

Jesse shrugged. "Maybe it's another one of Sophie's pranks."

"It's possible. But I think she's learned her lesson about pulling pranks and she was adamant that I needed to get here as quickly as—" She cut off when they passed Nothin' But Muffins. Her eyes widened.

Someone had painted the sign again. And not just with one *t*. They had completely painted over *Muffins* in white and had started writing something else in neat block letters.

Jesse finally noticed the sign and stopped the truck in the middle of the street. "Are you sure Sophie's done with pranks?"

"It wasn't her. The letters are too concise. Sophie is a messy painter. Whoever did this used a stencil." She read the sign. "Nothin' But LO'? What does that mean?"

"Nothin' But Lobster? Maybe the kid likes seafood and ran out of room."

She laughed. "Doubtful. Since the letters are capital, maybe it's an abbreviation for something. Kids nowadays love their texting abbreviations."

"Little Oddball?"

She rolled her eyes. "Don't ever become a contestant on *Wheel of Fortune*, Jess."

Jesse laughed as he pulled into a parking space in front of the sheriff's office. He turned off the engine and sent her an understanding look. "Do you want me to take care of this? You can wait in the truck if you aren't ready to see him."

Sunny shook her head. "I'll have to see him sooner or later." Besides, she was more than a little curious about what had caused strait-laced Reid Mitchell to get arrested—if he had gotten arrested and this wasn't one of Sophie's pranks.

Sunny didn't know what to expect when she pulled open the door of the sheriff's office, but it wasn't Decker sitting in Melba's chair holding Holly Joy in one arm and a tiny gray kitten in the other. Holly was squealing and waving her pudgy arms with excitement trying to get to the cat.

"Now, Holly," Decker said above the racket. "Remember what Mama said about bringing home more animals. So don't be gettin' too attached."

Holly released another squeal and clasped and unclasped her chubby fingers until Decker sighed. "Well, maybe one little kitten won't hurt anything."

Melba came out of the bathroom. "Of course a tiny kitten won't hurt anything. George Strait and Dixie Chick will love Loretta Lynn." She noticed Sunny standing by the door and smiled and winked at her before she held out her hands to Decker. "Give me Holly and put Loretta Lynn back in her crate. She needs to rest up before she meets those two ornery dogs of yours."

Decker handed the cute baby to Melba. "You aren't going to be happy until I have a zoo, are you, Mel?"

"Nothin' wrong with a zoo." Melba kissed Holly Joy's chubby cheek. "You just need to make sure you have lots of these sweet 'thangs' to help you take care of all your animals."

Decker shook his head as he put the cat back in the crate. When he was finished, he turned to Sunny. "I guess you're here to see our prisoner." He waved a hand. "Follow me."

Sunny was stunned when Decker led her down the hallway that led to the jail cell. "You really did lock up Reid? How could you do that, Decker? Reid's a good man. I'm sure whatever he did wasn't bad enough to be thrown in jail."

Decker stopped and glanced over his shoulder at her. "You didn't see the Nothin' But Muffins sign?"

She stared him. "Reid did that?"

He nodded before continuing down the hallway. "Caught him red handed after I got a call from Mrs. Stokes."

"But why?"

Decker unlocked the door at the end of the hallway and held it open for her. "I think you'll need to ask him yourself."

She stepped through the doorway and found Reid lying on the bottom bunk of the jail cell. When he saw her, he quickly rolled to his boots. Boots that were splattered with black paint. As were his T-shirt and jeans. His hair was messed like he'd been running his fingers through it and his eyes held too many emotions to read. Especially when she was feeling so many herself. Shock. Confusion. Heartache. And the overwhelming need to dive into his arms and never let him go.

Thankfully, the bars kept her from humiliating herself.

"W-W-Why?" she sputtered.

He shrugged. "It seemed to help get rid of the icky feelings for you and Sophie."

"You have icky feelings?"

He took a step closer. "I feel icky about the way I treated you. And I'm sorry, Sunny. I'm so damn sorry for taking my fear of losing Sophie out on you." He hesitated. "And it wasn't just my fear of losing Sophie that had me saying things I didn't mean. It was also my fear of losing you. Your parents might have made a lot of mistakes, but naming you wasn't one of them. You're like sunshine—warm, bright, and life giving. You certainly gave me new life. You burned away all the dark clouds surrounding me and made my world bright and shining. I'm terrified of losing that light. Even if you deserve better than an inept man who couldn't even paint a four-letter word and declare his true feelings to you without getting caught."

So *LO* wasn't an abbreviation. It was a word. The only four-letter word Sunny could think of that started with L and O had her heart beating faster as Reid continued.

"I know you already have plans to move to Dallas, but you don't belong in Dallas, Sunshine. You belong here with Corbin and Jesse and all the Holidays." He moved closer to the bars and grabbed on to them. "You belong here with me and Sophie. I might not have a lot to offer a woman who has everything, but I can offer you one thing. I can offer you my heart. If the hole in my chest is any indication, you already have it. I love you, Sunshine Whitlock. I have nothin' but love for you."

Nothin' But LOVE.

Sunny didn't know what to do or say. Responsible, law-abiding Reid had broken the law and committed a crime for her. To tell her, and the entire town, how he felt.

She couldn't hold back the tears even if she'd wanted to. They blurred her vision and splashed down her cheeks like heavy rain on a windshield. She heard the squeak of metal hinges before she was surrounded by male heat and hard muscle. Reid held her tightly as he brushed kisses on her head.

"I'm right here, baby. I'm right here."

She was enjoying the pure pleasure of releasing her emotions while being securely cocooned in Reid's strong arms when a thought struck her.

She drew back. "How did you get out?"

He grinned sheepishly. "It wasn't locked. I talked Decker into pretending like he locked me up because I knew if you saw me in jail, your big ol' heart would kick in and I'd have a better chance of winning you back."

"So you weren't arrested?"

"Nope. Thankfully, Decker believes in second chances . . . and true love." He leaned in to kiss her, but before he could, she punched him hard in the stomach. His eyes widened in shock as his breath came out in a startled woof.

"How dare you play such a trick on me, Reid Mitchell! You worried me half to death. And poor Sophie. She's probably back at the trailer wearing a hole in the rug, thinking you're going to jail and she's going to be parentless. I should kick your butt from one end of this town to the other." She might have socked him again if he hadn't wrapped her in his arms. His eyes were twinkling and his lips trembled with suppressed laughter.

Which made her even angrier.

"Just what is so funny, you lowdown lying snake?"

His smile broke free. "I've never seen you this mad before and you're mighty cute when you're ticked off."

"I'll show you cute." She struggled to get out of his arms, but it was like struggling to get out of a steel cage . . . one that was locked.

"Now calm down, honey. Sophie was in on it. And we only lied for one reason and that was to get you back where you belong." His arms tightened. "Right here in my arms. How can you be mad at that?"

"I'm mad because you tricked me when you could have just come to the bed-and-breakfast and told me how you feel."

"After the way I acted, I figured you deserved a bigger declaration. I'll climb up on a thousand roofs in the middle of the night and almost break my fool neck, paint a million signs, even go to jail. Whatever it takes to keep you from leaving. I don't plan on letting you go, Sunny Brook." He kissed the tip of her nose. "Ever."

With his words, the hard shell, that years of her parents' desertion had placed around her heart, melted like ice cream on a hot Texas sidewalk. She stopped struggling as tears gathered in her eyes.

"Well, why didn't you say that in the first place?" She looped her arms around his neck and kissed him. When she drew back, he was grinning from ear to ear.

"So you'll stay?"

She tried to act as nonchalant as possible, but it was hard when she was getting everything she ever wanted. Someone who loved her enough to never let her go. "Since you went to so much trouble to keep me, I guess it would be really mean to leave. And I'm just not a mean person."

Reid's eyes narrowed. "That's the only reason you're staying?"

"As you pointed out, there's my family. And

Sophie. And my gallery that I've decided to fill with my art."

"I'm happy for you, but there's not something you want to say to me?"

She pretended to think for a moment. "Umm ... nope."

He growled like the big grumpy bear he was. "Nope? Do you or don't you love me, Sunny Brook Whitlock?"

She released the smile she'd been holding. For the first time in a long time, she was smiling from the inside out. "You should already know the answer to that. I think I've made it pretty obvious that you've been stealing pieces of my heart ever since I first socked you in the arm at Thanksgiving."

"Even when I was a grieving grump?"

"Even then." She smoothed his hair back from his forehead. "I don't want a man who hides his true feelings. I want to know what you're feeling every moment of every day. And I'm not going to hide my true feelings from you either. I'm not all sunshine, Reid. I'm going to have grumpy days too. Can you handle that?"

"As long as you're by my side, Sunny, I can handle anything."

He kissed her.

It was filled with reverence and love and respect. She suddenly realized that all her life she had felt unworthy of love. From her parents. Her brothers. The kids at school. Even her Secret Sisters. But Reid had helped her realize that she *was* worthy. No matter how many pranks she'd pulled or how many fibs she'd told or how badly her paintings sold.

She deserved to be loved and cherished and never let go.

If the possessive way Reid held her was any indication, he intended to do just that.

And she intended to do the same.

She deepened the kiss and was seriously considering pushing him back into the jail cell to see how well they'd fit on the small bottom bunk when Sophie's exclamation had them jumping apart.

"Uncle Reid!"

Sunny turned to see Sophie standing in the doorway with Patsy Cline cradled in her arm and an exasperated look on her face.

"You didn't propose before I got here, did you?"

Sunny's gaze snapped to Reid. He didn't look at all surprised. In fact, he wore an extremely smug smile. "With an impressionable teenager in the house, I think it's our only choice."

"Of course it is." Sophie walked into the room, letting the door slam behind her. "Y'all don't want me thinking I can have sex without marriage, do you?" She set Patsy down and the rabbit started running laps in and out of the cell while Sophie gave Sunny a pleading look. "Say yes, Sunny. Please."

Sunny felt like her heart was going to burst right out of her chest. She fully intended to jump right back into Reid's arms and cover his face with kisses punctuated with yeses. But before she did . . .

"I have one condition."

Reid gave her a loving look. "Anything, baby."

She smiled wickedly. "You finish painting my sign."

Chapter Twenty-two

Sunny felt like she'd swallowed the sun and it radiated out from her in glowing rays of happiness.

Tomorrow, she was marrying a man who loved all of her. Her happy side and her sad side. Her sweet side and her angry side. Her calm side and her wild side. In the last month, Reid had witnessed it all.

Once Sunny had cracked open her emotions, they decided to put on quite a show. She had laughed more, cried more, and thrown more angry fits than she had in her life. She held nothing back from Reid and he hadn't gone anywhere.

At that very moment, he stood in front of "First Kiss" with a slight smile on his face as if he was reliving their first kiss through the abstract expressionism painting. A painting that hung with all the other angry art, along with her happier landscapes that he, Corbin, and Jesse had helped her bring back from Houston. While the gallery wasn't open yet, tonight was a preview for all her friends and family. It was slightly terrifying having pieces of herself on display, but it was also cathartic.

As she looked around, she realized this was who she was. Not just chaotic angry art, but also sedate country landscapes. A wild child and a sweet country gal.

"I can't believe you kept all these hidden, Sunny."

She turned to see Corbin standing there holding two glasses of Mimi's elderberry wine. Because what else would she have chosen to drink at her wedding rehearsal dinner?

She took a glass from him and took a sip, enjoying the tart, heady flavor. "I kept them hidden from myself, Cory. But everything is out now."

He studied her. "You sure? You're not keeping any more secrets from me?"

"Absolutely not. I'm through hiding my emotions and keeping secrets . . . well, only Secret Sister secrets. But you'll have to live with that."

He rolled his eyes and shook his head. "Yes, so Belle has told me."

"Speaking of secrets, when are you planning to tell Fiona Stokes about Ima Rhimes's letter?" Sunny had given him the letter weeks before and they'd both decided to wait to tell Mrs. Stokes, or anyone for that matter, until the investigator Corbin hired could get them more information.

Corbin's expression saddened. "I don't know that I am. The investigator discovered that Ima passed away in Oklahoma City at the age of thirty-seven. She had a daughter. Unfortunately, the daughter went into foster care after her death and those files are closed. It seems hurtful to bring up Mrs. Stokes's father's infidelity if I can't locate her sister."

Sunny didn't agree. "But wouldn't you have wanted to know that Jesse existed? Even if we never found him? I would have. And I know you, Cory. You're as stubborn as the day is long and you never would have given up looking for him. Just like Jesse never gave up looking for us." They both glanced over at Jesse who was talking with Rome and Casey Remington with his usual goofy grin. "Siblings are worth fighting for." Sunny smiled at Corbin. "You've taught me that."

Corbin pulled her in for a tight hug. "Okay. I'll give Mrs. Stokes the letter after the wedding. Maybe I'll give her one of those DNA ancestry test kits with it and we'll see if we can locate her sister that way."

"You're a good man, Corbin Whitlock." Sunny gave him a kiss on the cheek. "And speaking of good men, I'm going to go find my fiancé."

But before she could reach Reid, she ran into her sisters. They were standing in front of Sunny's most recent painting, a chaotic mixture of blue splashes with a white luminous ball hanging above seven vibrant pink splatters. "Full Moon Sisters" was one of her favorite paintings. Which was why it wasn't for sale. After the grand opening of the gallery, she would hang it and "First Kiss" in the trailer until she and Reid built a house on the five-hundred acres of land Corbin had given them for their wedding gift.

It looked like Reid would get his ranch after all.

And Sunny would get her dream of living on the Holiday Ranch.

As Mimi always liked to say, *Things work out if you let them.*

"Sunny!" Noelle hooked an arm through hers. "I'm glad you showed up. We have an emergency."

Hallie huffed an exasperated sigh. "Once again, Elle has ordered a bridesmaid's dress that's too small for her."

"I can't help it if I've gotten a little bigger since I ordered the dress. In case you forgot, Hal, I'm pregnant!"

"How could I forget when it's all you ever talk about? I'm so sick of hearing about the cradle Casey is making you and how he calls the baby 'Sugar Muffin' and your detailed plans for the 'cutest little ranch room,' I could puke."

"I hate to point this out," Liberty said. "But you puke at the drop of a hat, Hal. And I believe I overheard Jace calling your baby bump 'Teenier Weeny.' Which is pretty pukeworthy." She rubbed her huge stomach. "Besides, my bridesmaid's dress is a little snug too."

"Because you're the size of the Goodyear Blimp."

Liberty's eyes narrowed. "Oh, you just wait, Hallie Carson. The shorter the waist, the bigger the belly."

"What?" Noelle looked horrified as she placed a hand on her rounded stomach. "That means I'm going to look like a beach ball with shoes."

Belle patted Noelle's shoulder. "Every woman carries babies differently, Elle. Just look at me and Libby."

Liberty stared at her twin. "And just what does that mean, Belly?"

Before Belle had to answer, Cloe stepped in. "What Belly means is that every pregnant woman is stunning in her own way. Now let's focus on finding a solution for the problem at hand."

"Cloe's right," Sweetie said. "And lucky for us, we have a grandmother who sews." She looked over at Mimi who was talking to Darla and Hank. "Mimi! We need you."

Mimi looked more than a little skeptical when she arrived. "Just what mischief are y'all up to now?"

"We have a dress situation," Cloe said. "Do you think you could alter Noelle's dress before the wedding tomorrow?"

"And mine," Liberty said.

"And mine," Hallie said. When all the sisters turned to her, she shrugged. "What? I might have gained a little pregnancy weight too!"

Everyone laughed and Mimi patted Hallie's arm. "Yes. I'll get to yours too, Halloween." She shook her head. "Y'all should thank your lucky stars that your great-grandma taught me how to sew. Ima altered wedding dresses for blushing young brides until the day she died. God rest her sweet soul."

Sunny stared at Mimi. "Your mama's name was Ima?"

"Ima Lee Rhimes. Best mama a woman could ever ask for."

Reid was as nervous as a dog on bath day. He was more than thankful Sunny hadn't wanted a formal wedding. He would have died from heatstroke in a tuxedo jacket. Even in a cotton western shirt and jeans, he was burning up. And that was in an air-conditioned house. Once he got in the barn, he would be a walking sweat ball.

"Here."

He turned to see his best man holding out a bandana. He took it from Corbin and wiped the sweat from his forehead. "Just so you know, this has nothing to do with me getting cold feet. There's nothing more I want than to marry your sister. I'm just . . ." He struggled to find the right words. Corbin helped him out.

"Worried about being enough. Believe me, I get it. I was terrified about the same thing when I married Belle. She was everything good and I was—"

Jesse, who was sprawled out on the twin bed in one of the Holidays' upstairs guestrooms with Buck snoozing on his chest, cut his brother off. "A grudge-holding asshole."

Corbin shot him an annoyed look. "Thanks, Jess."

Jesse grinned. "Just trying to keep it real, Whitty." He glanced at Reid. "I was nervous too. I still wonder how in the hell I got so lucky."

"Every single day." Decker sat on the opposite bed, watching his new kitten, Loretta Lynn, play with Tay-Tay on the carpeted cat condo that stood in the window. Jelly Roll, Jace and Hallie's cat, was sitting on the very top looking down at the young kittens with disdainful eyes.

"Try every single second." Jace walked into the room, carrying a cooler of beer. No doubt homebrewed by Hallie. Once he finished passing out the bottles, Rome spoke.

"What we're trying to say, Reid, is that we've all been in your shoes. We've all felt the same insecurities about marrying strong women with high expectations. The question is . . . are you going to let a few insecurities keep you from marrying the best thing that will ever happen to you in your life?"

Reid didn't hesitate. "Hell, no."

Casey slapped him on the back. "Good man!" He held up his beer and grinned. "To the Holiday sisters' men. We're some lucky bastards."

"Hear! Hear!" all the men chorused.

Reid had barely taken a sip when Sophie walked in. She looked stunning in her pale yellow maid-of-honor dress with her makeup applied perfectly. She also looked way too grown up. Reid couldn't help but feel a pang of sadness. A few months ago, he couldn't wait for her to grow up. Now, just the thought of her leaving for college made him want to bawl like a baby.

"Y'all about ready to head down to the barn?" she asked as she looked around at the men.

Everyone took another guzzle of their beers before they set them back in the cooler and filed out. Reid held out his arm for Sophie.

"You look beautiful, Soph."

She beamed. "Thank you, Uncle Reid. Just wait until you see Sunny."

Sophie wasn't exaggerating. When Reid saw Sunny standing in the doorway of the Holidays' barn, his heart felt like it took flight. She looked like an angel in her simple white dress with her golden-red hair surrounding her shoulders in soft waves.

She even had a set of wings.

Jimmy Buffett was perched on her shoulder. In the last couple months, the parrot had become extremely attached to Sunny. He spent most of his time sitting on her shoulder . . . and cussing up a storm. Although today he seemed to be on his best behavior. Or maybe the mini bow tie around his neck was just too tight. Whatever the reason, he merely nodded his head when Hank Holiday handed Sunny off to Reid.

The love in her warm brown eyes made all Reid's nerves vanish.

He didn't know how he'd gotten so lucky, but he wasn't going to question his luck. He was just going to hold on to it with both hands. As soon as Sunny gave her bouquet and Jimmy Buffet to Sophie, he took her hands in his and held firmly.

Sunny squeezed back and smiled a smile that was as real as the love he had in his heart for this woman. "You ready to get hitched to me for life?"

He grinned. "Baby, I was born ready."
"Bullshit!" Jimmy Buffett squawked.

Epilogue

THE HARVEST MOON was the biggest Fiona had ever seen in her life.

It hung in the night sky like a huge golden coin, illuminating Cooper Springs and the naked nymphs who frolicked in the shimmering water. Although not all of the nymphs were frolicking. Fiona and Mimi had left the frolicking to Darla, Sunny, Sophie, and the Holiday sisters while they floated in the shallows and watched.

In the last year, the Secret Sisterhood had grown from seven to eleven. The meetings were held the second Thursday night of every month in the Holiday barn hayloft. Due to the men worrying about pregnant wives and old women falling down the ladder, last Christmas, the men had surprised the sisters with a completely redecorated loft with railed stairs, new lighting, a plush rug, comfortable sofas and chairs . . . and a mini wine fridge filled with Hallie's homemade beer and Mimi's elderberry wine.

Which explained why all the sisters—except for Sophie who only got to drink Mountain Dew—were a wee bit tipsy now.

"Watch this!" Hallie yelled as she grabbed on to the rope Jace and Decker had tied to a low-hanging limb on Fourth of July. Since Casey had promptly broken his arm while testing the rope to make sure it was secure, Fiona couldn't help yelling out a warning . . . at the exact same time as Mimi.

"No flips, Hal!"

Mimi and Fiona looked at each other and smiled. It wasn't the first time they had spoken the exact same thing at the exact same time. No doubt due to all the time they'd spent together in the last year.

They had always been friends who enjoyed each other's company when they saw each other at parties, book club, town council meetings, or church gatherings. But since finding out they were half-sisters, they had become more than just friends.

They had become inseparable.

If Mimi wasn't at Fiona's house, Fiona was at the Holiday Ranch. They had a lot of time to make up for . . . and not nearly enough time left to do it. Which was why Fiona was considering Mimi's offer to come live at the Holiday Ranch. She had always wanted a big family and now it looked like she had one.

She was Aunt Fifi. A title she pretended not to like, but secretly loved.

Since finding her family, she'd even considered retiring. But after taking a week off to help Mimi with her gardening, she vetoed the idea. She was a woman who enjoyed going to an office and being in charge. She figured she'd run her own businesses for as long as the good Lord let her. When she couldn't anymore, she planned to sell out and donate the money to charity.

She glanced out at the springs.

The Holidays didn't need money.

Their cups already runneth over.

And so did Fiona's. She thanked God every day for bringing Mimi to Wilder. Ima had kept her word to Mrs. Fields and never told her daughter who her father was. But she *had* told her daughter about a quaint Texas town where she'd once lived. It had been enough to get Mimi here. Falling in love with a Holiday had done the rest.

And if that wasn't God's plan, Fiona didn't know what was.

"What are you thinking about, Fi?" Mimi asked as she floated on her back and looked up at the full moon.

She joined her sister in a float and took her hand. "How blessed we are."

Mimi squeezed her hand. "That we are. There was a point where I thought all was lost. The ranch. My granddaughters. Now everyone is home where they belong and happily married with babies. Seven little girls to carry on the Holiday Ranch."

Fiona didn't doubt for a second that they would.

They might just be babies, and Sunny and Reid's daughter only two months old, but Fiona could already tell that Holly Joy, Autumn Grace, Valentine Rose, America Hope, Glory Faith, Luna Catalina, and Spring Blossom were all going to be strong-willed, capable women like their mamas.

Mimi sighed with contentment. "Even in my dreams, I couldn't have imagined a better happily-ever-after."

Fiona had to agree. She had never thought in a million years that she'd have a sister and a big loving family.

"I guess that's life for you, Mi," she said. "It's full of surprises."

"It certainly is, Fi." Mimi came up out of her float, her eyes glittering with mischief. "Have you ever tried a rope swing?"

THE END

Turn the page for an excerpt of Katie Lane's western fairytale series, Kingman Ranch!

Charming a Texas Beast
is available now for FREE!

Sneak Peek!

Charming a Texas Beast

Chapter One

THE TOWN OF Cursed, Texas, came by its name honestly.

Droughts, pestilence, dust storms, floods, tornados, Indians, and outlaws beset the first settlers. That was just in the first year. A large percentage of the pioneers gave up and moved on, hoping to find a more welcoming place to settle. Only the hardest, toughest, and most stubborn folks stayed. Honest folks who believed in calling a spade a spade. They weren't about to call their unlucky town Blessed.

Over the years, things didn't get much better. It became a badge of honor to live in Cursed. The townsfolk were quite proud of being the type of people who could survive anything.

Not only survive but thrive.

Although as Lillian Leigh Daltry drove through Cursed, it didn't look like her hometown was thriving. The old gas station had only one working pump. The restaurant was in a crumbling building with a faded sign on one wall that said Good Eats. And Nasty Jack's bar still had no sign at all, blacked out windows, and a hitching post in front. Even with the storm brewing overhead, there were three horses tied to the hitching post—and more than a dozen dusty trucks parked in the lot.

The post office, feed store, and small grocery store weren't as run-down, but they were in need of renovations. Only the business at the end of the main street looked prosperous. The rambling farmhouse was painted a pristine white with pretty navy-blue shutters and a bright red door. In the living room window a neon sign hung: *Fortunetelling and Palm Reading.* In a town that was cursed, fortunetellers and palm readers were an absolute must.

As was a church.

Holy Gossip with its sky-high bell tower was the biggest building in town.

Just not the biggest building in the county.

Kingman Ranch held that honor. While the town was cursed, the Kingmans had been more than blessed. They owned one of the biggest ranches in Texas and had built a castle to prove it. The townsfolk of Cursed referred to the huge mansion in many different ways: Bucking-Horse Palace. Kingman's Folly. Western Camelot. Cowboy Castle. And One Big-Assed House. But Lily had always thought of the massive house with its multiple turrets in only one way.

Home.

Not that Lily had ever lived in the sprawling stone structure with its cultured marble bathrooms, dining room table that could seat half the congregation of Holy Gossip, and its basement with the bar bigger than the one at Nasty Jack's. But she had lived in the gardener's cottage just a short distance from the main house. She'd lived there with her loving parents, who'd been the Kingmans' gardeners until her mother passed away. Then she'd lived there with her father . . . until she'd turned eighteen and completely humiliated herself.

Lily's face still heated with embarrassment every time she thought of that night. But she wasn't a naïve teenager anymore. She was a successful, mature woman who was no longer starstruck by a handsome prince cowboy who lived in a Texas castle.

Which didn't explain why her heart added an extra beat and her sweaty hands clenched the steering wheel of the rental car as she turned off the highway and drove under the stone entrance to the Kingman Ranch with its two sculpted rearing stallions. When she rounded a bend and the castle came into view, her anxiety increased tenfold.

The mansion didn't look like a fairytale castle tonight. Angry, black clouds completely obliterated the moon and stars. The pitch-black night, lit only by the occasional bolt of jagged lightning, made the house look less like Cinderella's castle and more like Dr. Frankenstein's. It had yet to rain. But Lily knew the skies were only moments away from releasing a torrent, so she wasted no time driving over the pond bridge and circling around the large house to the cottage in back.

While the Kingman house was big and grand, the cottage was small and quaint. Her mother had designed the river rock house and it looked like it belonged in the English countryside rather than on a Texas ranch. The roof was steep and shingled with cedar and the windows were multi-paned with brightly painted boxes beneath that held a flourish of spring flowers.

Grief consumed Lily at just the sight of her beloved home. Or maybe what caused her grief was that Gwen Daltry was no longer inside to greet her with a tight hug and warm English biscuits straight from the oven. She was no longer there to tenderly brush Lily's hair and tell her she was the most talented, beautiful girl in the world. She was no longer there to hear about her daughter's greatest accomplishments . . . or her worst fears.

While Lily loved her father, they had never had the close connection she and her mother had. Theodore Daltry was a quiet man who kept his thoughts to himself. Similar to Lily. Gwen had been the outgoing and gregarious one in the family. The one who made every day sparkle. With her gone, the cottage had lost all its life. Now it was just a place Lily had once lived.

A boom of thunder split the night, startling her out of her thoughts. She quickly pulled next to the cottage and got out. Since it was so late, she didn't expect her father to be waiting up—especially when he was on painkillers for his broken leg. But she had expected him to leave a light on and the door unlocked. The cottage was dark, and both the front and back doors were bolted tight. Which was odd. The doors had never been locked when she'd lived there. There was no need. Everyone who worked on the ranch was trusted.

She knocked on the door. "Daddy? It's Lily."

When her father didn't answer, she began to grow concerned. She grew even more concerned when she called his cell phone and it went straight to voice mail. Another clap of thunder had her jumping. A second later the skies opened, and rain poured down. She had wanted to avoid the Kingman family as much as possible while taking care of her father, but now she had no choice. They would know where her father was or have a key to the cottage. Hopefully, her father wasn't inside and unable to answer the door or phone.

With rain pummeling her, she hurried along the brick path that led to the back door of the Kingman castle. One of her spiked heels got caught in a crack between bricks and she went down hard, ripping her dress and scraping one knee. By the time she reached the door, she was a hot mess. So much for returning home looking like a mature, successful woman. But worry for her father overrode her ego, and she pounded on the sturdy oak door with its bronze Texas star. When minutes passed and no one answered, she tried the doorknob. Thankfully, it was unlocked.

As a child, she'd been scared to enter the house at night. The high, echoing ceilings and long, dark hallways had her imagination running wild with images of ghosts and ghouls. Now, the only fear she had was for her father.

"Hello?" she called as she stepped into the mudroom. "Anyone home?"

She flipped the light switch, but nothing happened. The flashlight on her phone didn't work either. She couldn't even get the screen to come up. She'd obviously broken it when she fell. She placed the phone on a bench by the door and moved into the dark kitchen. A flickering light drew her across the grand foyer into the main living area.

A fire burned low in the massive floor-to-ceiling Austin stone fireplace. No one seemed to be enjoying the deep orange glow of the dying embers, but it looked as if someone had been. A half glass of amber liquid and an open book sat on a table next to a huge chair made of cowhide leather.

The Kingman throne.

The patriarch of the Kingman family, Charlie Kingman, or King as he'd been called, had sat in that very chair while presiding over family gatherings. Lily had been too little to remember much about the man. All she remembered was that he'd been big, mean, and bossy. After he'd passed away, his son, Douglas, had presided over the ranch. But Douglas had never sat in the chair. Maybe because he'd been a much smaller, nicer man who had felt uncomfortable sitting in the pretentious piece of furniture.

But when he passed away, his son Stetson had no problem taking over the Kingman throne. Or filling his grandfather's boots. Stetson was just as much of an arrogant beast as his grandfather had been. And just another reason Lily had stayed away from the ranch until now.

Turning from the fire, she headed down the hallway to the grand staircase that led to the bedrooms. She hated to wake the entire house, but she was willing to do whatever it took to find her father.

As she climbed the curved marble stairs, a chill of remembrance ran through her. She had followed the same path on her high school graduation night. But she hadn't been looking for her father that night. She'd been looking for Stetson's brother Wolfe Kingman, the boy who had starred in all her fantasies since she was old enough to feel the first stirrings of sexual awareness. Wolfe, whose handsome face made her heart beat faster and her knees turn to water. Wolfe, who always had a wink and a smile to give the gardener's shy daughter.

The soft click of boot heels on marble stairs startled her out of her thoughts. She whirled and the wet soles of her shoes slipped. She might have plummeted to her death if she hadn't been stopped by what felt like a solid brick wall.

But the arms that encircled her weren't made of brick. They were made of hard muscle and warm skin. They easily caught her and lifted her against an even harder chest. It was too dark to see his face. But she didn't need to. Her body had only reacted this way to one man.

Wolfe.

Anger that a man she hadn't seen in close to eight years could make her heart flutter and her pulse race had her stiffening in his arms and speaking sharply. "Put me down."

He didn't answer. His arms tightened and he carried her down the stairs as she tried not to notice the flex of his muscles and the warmth of his bare skin. When they reached the bottom, she expected him to set her on her feet. Instead, he carried her into the living room and placed her in King's chair.

When he stepped back, she drew in a sharp breath. He wasn't the prince charming she expected.

He was the beast.

Stetson.

The shadows cast by the dying embers emphasized the hard angles of his face, his deep-set eyes, and the faint white scars that covered his left cheek. Lily didn't know how the oldest Kingman had gotten the scars and she'd always been too terrified of Stetson to ask.

And with due cause.

"What the hell are you doing sneaking around in the dark?" he growled. "If you had fallen down those stairs, you could've broken your fool neck."

When she was little, she'd always burst into tears and run away whenever Stetson got after her. But she was no longer a scared little girl . . . at least, that's what she kept telling herself.

She stiffened her spine and met his hard gaze head on. "I wouldn't have startled and almost fallen if you hadn't snuck up behind me. And I wasn't sneaking around in your house. I knocked on the door, but no one answered."

"So you just came right in?"

"Your father made sure everyone knew they could always come right in. Obviously, you don't put out the same welcome mat."

Stetson leaned closer, the glowing embers reflecting in his polished onyx eyes. "Sometimes it's not a good idea to walk into people's houses without an invitation, Goldilocks. I thought you would've learned that the night you tried to sneak into Wolfe's bed."

Her face flamed with embarrassment. She had hoped Stetson would have forgotten that night. She should've known better. He wasn't the type of man who forgot things . . . or let them go.

She pushed down her humiliation and got to the reason for her visit. "I'm looking for my father. I went to the cottage, but the doors are locked and he wouldn't answer my knock or the phone."

"Because he's here. When the power went out, I thought he'd be safer in the guest room."

Her shoulders relaxed and she leaned her head back against the chair and closed her eyes. "Thank God. I worried he was lying inside the cottage unable to move or wandering around in this storm delusional from the pain medication the doctor gave him." A snort had her eyes flashing open. Even in the low light, it was easy to read the contempt on Stetson's face.

"You were worried? Since when do you care about your father, Lillian Leigh?"

Disbelief and anger had her sitting straight up. "Excuse me?"

He cocked his head and stared down at her. Had he gotten even taller and more muscular or was it just a trick of the shadows from the glowing firelight? "Do I have it wrong? Have you been secretly visiting your daddy and I wasn't aware of it? Because I haven't seen you anywhere around for the last eight years. You weren't here when he caught the flu and was in bed for a week. You weren't here when he cut his hand sharpening his hedge trimmers and had to have twelve stitches. You weren't here when he fell off a ladder and broke his leg in two places. And you sure haven't been here for any holidays, birthdays, or your mother's birthdays and the anniversary of her death when your father takes flowers to her grave . . . alone."

Lily hadn't known about her father's illness or his accident with the hedge trimmers. Both upset her. But what caused a hard lump of emotion to form in her throat was the thought of him going to her mother's grave site. Alone.

"And yet all he does is brag about you," Stetson continued. "He bursts with pride every time he shows me a book you just released or a children's writers' award you won."

Her father was proud of her? Why had he never told her? Probably the same reason he hadn't told her about his accidents, illnesses, and visits to the cemetery. She wouldn't have known that he broke his leg if the doctor hadn't called her because she was listed as his next of kin. And yet, it seemed he had no trouble talking to Stetson.

That hurt. It hurt a lot. But Stetson had always known exactly what to say to hurt her.

He wasn't done yet.

"What makes absolutely no sense to me is that you have all the time in the world for your writing, but you can't make time to come see your own father. In my book, that's nothing but selfishness."

She wanted to argue, but the truth of Stetson's words cut right through her. Tears of guilt filled her eyes. She tried to blink them away. When she couldn't, she jumped up and headed for the door.

It seemed that things at the Kingman Ranch hadn't changed after all.

Stetson could still make her cry.

―――

Get ***Charming a Texas Beast***
absolutely FREE today!

https://tinyurl.com/2u3syjn2

Acknowledgments

Where did the time go? I feel like I just started the Holiday Ranch series and now it's time to say goodbye to my beloved town and characters . . . and thank all the amazing folks who helped me get the seven Holiday sister's stories into your hot little hands.

Lindsey Faber. I don't know how I lucked out getting one of the best editors in the business, but every day I thank my lucky stars for you. Your insights on how to make my books better are always spot-on perfect.

Immi Howson. I sleep much better every night knowing I can make mistakes with my grammar, timeline, and characters and you'll catch them before my books go out into the world.

Speaking of getting my books out into the world, I couldn't without you, Jennifer Jakes. If I need anything—formatting, cover copy, just a little pat on the back and words of encouragement—you have always been right there to lend your expertise, creative brain, and support.

Kim Killion, cover designer extraordinaire. Thank you for making my covers so eye-catching and gorgeous . . . and putting up with my nitpicking.

And last, but certainly not least, I need to thank my readers. Your love and support is what keeps me tapping away on the worn-out keys of my laptop. Yes, I probably should get a new one, but I'm the type of person who gets attached to things and refuses to let them go. Laptops, coffee mugs, sweaters, cars . . . my readers. That's right. Now that I got you, I'm not gonna let you go. Stay tuned for another small Texas town romance series filled with spunky heroines, charming heroes, and lovable townsfolk!

Love,
Katie

Also by Katie Lane

Be sure to check out all of Katie Lane's novels!
www.katielanebooks.com

~

Holiday Ranch Series
Wrangling a Texas Sweetheart
Wrangling a Lucky Cowboy
Wrangling a Texas Firecracker
Wrangling a Hot Summer Cowboy
Wrangling a Texas Hometown Hero
Wrangling a Christmas Cowboy
Wrangling a Wild Texan

Kingman Ranch Series
Charming a Texas Beast
Charming a Knight in Cowboy Boots
Charming a Big Bad Texan
Charming a Fairytale Cowboy
Charming a Texas Prince
Charming a Christmas Texan
Charming a Cowboy King

Bad Boy Ranch Series:
Taming a Texas Bad Boy
Taming a Texas Rebel
Taming a Texas Charmer

Taming a Texas Heartbreaker
Taming a Texas Devil
Taming a Texas Rascal
Taming a Texas Tease
Taming a Texas Christmas Cowboy

Brides of Bliss Texas Series:

Spring Texas Bride
Summer Texas Bride
Autumn Texas Bride
Christmas Texas Bride

Tender Heart Texas Series:

Falling for Tender Heart
Falling Head Over Boots
Falling for a Texas Hellion
Falling for a Cowboy's Smile
Falling for a Christmas Cowboy

Deep in the Heart of Texas Series:

Going Cowboy Crazy
Make Mine a Bad Boy
Catch Me a Cowboy
Trouble in Texas
Flirting with Texas
A Match Made in Texas
The Last Cowboy in Texas
My Big Fat Texas Wedding

Overnight Billionaires Series:

A Billionaire Between the Sheets
A Billionaire After Dark
Waking up with a Billionaire

Hunk for the Holidays Series:
Hunk for the Holidays
Ring in the Holidays
Unwrapped

About the Author

KATIE LANE IS a firm believer that love conquers all and laughter is the best medicine. Which is why you'll find plenty of humor and happily-ever-afters in her contemporary and western contemporary romance novels. A USA Today Bestselling Author, she has written numerous series, including *Deep in the Heart of Texas, Hunk for the Holidays, Overnight Billionaires, Tender Heart Texas, The Brides of Bliss Texas, Bad Boy Ranch, Kingman Ranch,* and *Holiday Ranch.* Katie lives in Albuquerque, New Mexico, and when she's not writing, she enjoys reading, eating chocolate (dark, please), and snuggling with her high school sweetheart and cairn terrier, Roo.

For more on her writing life or just to chat, check out Katie here:
FACEBOOK
www.facebook.com/katielaneauthor
INSTAGRAM
www.instagram.com/katielanebooks.

And for more information on upcoming releases and great giveaways, be sure to sign up for her mailing list at www.katielanebooks.com!

Printed in Great Britain
by Amazon